RAGS &
REMINDERS

*Warmest thanks
Chris !*

Alan Wright

Alan

Michael Terence
Publishing

Lord's 6/18

First published in paperback by
Michael Terence Publishing in 2017
www.mtp.agency

ISBN 9781973164678

RAGS &
REMINDERS

Alan Wright

Warmest thanks to everyone I've met during my speaking and broadcasting career over the last thirty years or so – and for so much fun and friendship along the way.

CHAPTER 1 – PRESENT TIME

There are days which start well and for Janet Bremner this was one of them.

Just after ten in the morning, and a whole day and more stretching ahead to do as she wished.

For a woman who'd been married for twenty years, that shouldn't sound like an achievement, but it was.

John was out of the house and wouldn't be back till late tomorrow from a speaking gig in London.

Janet could read, do crosswords, watch soaps, drink wine – whatever – without a presence suggesting that she should be doing something more useful.

Feet up, coffee and biscuits at hand.

Then, at twenty past ten precisely, the phone rang.

Bless modern technology for inventing caller display which would probably prove that this was yet another call from some idiot announcing, "this is a free message" like there was another kind.

This time, though, a name flashed up, but it was unlikely to be more than a thirty second interruption.

Brian – the accountant – was the name on screen, and it was John, not her, who handled all that stuff.

"Hi Brian," said Janet, "you've missed him", he's just gone off to speak in London – it's a biggie in Park Lane."

"I know" said Brian "it's you I need to talk to."

"Can you come into the office to have a chat about something on my desk?"

No attempt at a double entendre, no nothing, this was

business.

"What is it?" was the best reply she could manage.

"It's a cheque for ten million pounds - made payable to you."

"What do I have that's worth ten million quid to anybody?"

"John" came the reply.

CHAPTER 2 - 1982

John's path to becoming a much travelled and highly paid speaker began in very different surroundings to the five-star hotels and top end cruise ships which became his normal life.

It all started in a world which has almost, but not quite, gone.

It was all so different back then, and the past, in working men's clubs in the north east of England, was very much a foreign country.

Many of the frequent attendees were indeed working men, or had been, and, on some nights would even take along their wives.

Some nights, though, were very much of the stag variety and had a pretty standard formula of a couple of comedians and three or four strippers - with pie and peas often included to lend a bit of class.

For reasons lost in the mists of time, another essential ingredient was a duo of drummer and organist who would provide live play-on music for the comedian and, bizarrely, random tunes for the strippers.

Recorded music and backing tracks would soon eliminate the handy extra earner for the musicians, but, in 1977, the live duo was in steady demand.

Many of these twosomes were handy musical talents, but, until the Royal Philharmonic came calling, a brown envelope of ready cash was not to be sniffed at.

Thus it was that John received an unexpected invitation which kicked off a life change.

His old friend Terry phoned around tea time and asked if he was free that night.

He was, and Janet was due to be out living it up at a Tupperware party.

Terry explained that he was playing the organ that night, with drummer friend Alan, at a "gala gentlemen's evening" in a local workies' club.

The gala would include the standard menu of gags, strippers and pies and sounded splendid.

When they arrived just before seven, the club was already beginning to fill and, even on a weekday evening, it looked like the grandly named "concert room" would be packed.

The man at the table on the door asked the party of three if they were members, which they weren't, or if they were "affiliated".

This question would often completely throw the rare southern visitor, but it was simply a query which checked if you were a member of another workies' club, which would give you a member's right of entrance for the night.

Terry proudly announced, "we're the band" and so John headed with them into the privileged world of the "artistes' room" backstage.

This was an extended broom cupboard, including brooms, where the musicians would put on their bow ties, the comedians would check their gags, and the strippers would put their kit on and off with pretty much nil attention.

This shoebox of a room made movement difficult at the best of times but it was even worse tonight because of the unusual sight of a man trying to balance a large bass drum on his back and a pair of cymbals between his knees.

The one-man band was having something of a resurgence after the one hit wonder of Rosie performed by Don Partridge.

He'd had, for a busker, the rare experience of a big hit parade success back in 1968, and several entertainers like tonight's specimen thought that success was just around their corner too. It wasn't.

The man charged with stage managing this lot was short and tubby Stan, the grandly named concert secretary, who booked the acts and acted as compere for the evening.

Totally unsuited to the job of comedy impresario, as he didn't like laughing much, he was also largely disliked by artistes and club members alike as he was an arrogant git, with delusions of adequacy.

He stuck his head into the room and scanned the assembled cast.

He nodded to the strippers and the band, whom he knew, grunted at John, whom he didn't, and then his eyes fell on the one-man band.

"Who the fuck are you?" he enquired.

"I'm Gerry Walsh, one-man band extraordinaire."

"I didn't book you, you daft bastard." countered Stan.

"Yes you did." replied cymbal man, "I have my booking letter from the agent here", trying to reach into an inside pocket blocked by a frame holding a kazoo, a small trumpet and a mini saxophone.

"Your agent's a daft bastard too" said Stan, "I booked Gary Welsh the blue comedian."

"He's in Doncaster tonight" said Gerry as he wriggled past the kazoo frame to show the letter to prove that it was indeed Stan who was the aforesaid daft bastard and had booked the similar sounding but totally wrong man.

"Well, you'll have to go on in the first slot" said Stan, thinking on his feet.

"No problem" lied Gerry, as his knocking knees produced a highly inappropriate cymbal clash, perfectly in time with a great farting noise from the kazoo as he replaced the vital letter.

Also thinking on his feet, Gerry insisted that the compere would tell the audience that he was indeed a one-man band and didn't know any gags, blue or otherwise.

A look of panic came back to Stan's face as he realised that the top of the bill comedian wasn't there either.

"And where the flying arseholes is Kenny Ricketts?" he asked everyone and no-one in particular.

No answer came, so it was decided that it was OK to await his arrival until the interval just before the pie and peas.

Stan decided that it was high time that the show was moving as there were now nearly a thousand punters packed into the concert room, their loins and chuckle muscles fired up by a few pints.

The band shuffled on to their keyboard and drums and played a few tunes to a response of total apathy,

John shuffled round to one wing and looked across

past the duo to Gerry the one-man band who was standing in the opposite wing shaking his head and wondering what sin he'd committed in a former life to deserve an evening like this.

The band finished, shuffled off, and were totally ignored.

On came Stan who thanked the band and promised that they'd be back soon to accompany the "exotic dancers."

"And now gentlemen," he continued, "would you please welcome one of the best blue comedians in clubland today - let's have a huge round of applause for the one and only Gary Walsh!"

Gerry, not Gary, shook his head even harder in the opposite wing and turned white.

He shuffled on with his instruments strapped around him and was greeted by the unusual sound of a thousand cheering voices dropping to bemused silence in a split second.

Echoing Stan's earlier words, one thousand people wondered who the fuck he was.

To his eternal credit, Gerry gave a performance of Rosie which Mr Partridge would have been proud of, and finished to a sprinkling of applause reminiscent of a four being scored at a village cricket match.

His next number, which usually worked well with an audience not expecting wall to wall filth, involved getting a volunteer from the audience to join him on stage and try his hand with a mini one-man band outfit.

A gently inebriated volunteer came up from the front row and strapped on the child size musical kit.

"And where are you from?" asked Gerry, using his best audience participation patter.

"From down there, you daft bastard" replied audience man, to the first big laugh of the night.

Gerry had now been called a daft bastard, orally and mentally, many times in the last few minutes and was in total agreement.

Ever a pro, he completed his planned set, walked off to more apathy, and was greeted by Stan in the wings who gave him the kind of review you don't often see in the arts pages of the Guardian, "You were shite son."

It's traditional for comperes to come on stage and thank the departing artist, but Stan was cut from a different cloth.

"Sorry lads" he said, "he was shite."

In the wings, the shitey daft bastard was packing up his gear and thinking that if his next gig was a social night in Hell, it would be a bigger success.

Still in the wings, John and the band were stuffing hankies in their mouths and weeping silent tears of laughter.

John was left alone, as the band shuffled back on stage, ready to play backing music for the next artiste.

Cheering up, Stan bellowed into the mike that he was now delighted to welcome a real entertainer, always welcome at this club, the amazing Lola.

Peering through a chink in his wing curtain John was puzzled to see some of the older guys at the front taking off their jackets and putting them on again, back to front.

He soon found out why.

Lola the stripper had already done a few laps of the stage and the audience and was now down to a tiny pair of pants, and an eye boggling display of enormous and swinging knockers.

She returned to the stage, picked up a bottle of golden brown suntan oil, and smeared it over the said hooters.

Back in the audience, she spotted a young man in a pristine white shirt who was clearly new to these evenings.

"Let's have a cuddle" said Lola, and the young chap stood up, beaming a huge smile at his cheering mates.

The jacket protection of the more experienced Lola fans now made sense, as two enormous tit prints were left on the young innocent's shirt. "Explain that to your lass when you get home" shouted a friend, and that would indeed be a challenge.

Lola finished her act, took a bow and went off to sustained applause, heard in the car park by the one man band who was packing his gear into the boot of his car.

Fat Stan appeared on stage and thanked Lola before announcing the best news of the night – the pies had arrived.

He left his audience queuing for food and bingo cards and went backstage to check things out for the second half.

The broom cupboard "green room" was now comparatively spacious as the one-man band had departed.

It was too spacious, though, as Kenny, the top of the bill comedian, had not appeared.

The total population of the artistes' room was the two-man band, John, and the final stripper of the night.

"Bollocks" exclaimed Stan, who ran to the phone to check why his star performer had not appeared.

He came back in some distress as there was no answer from the agent's phone and, in those far off pre-mobile phone days, he could only presume that the comedian's car had broken down en route.

Either way, he was stuffed, and expressed as much to the assembled broom cupboard crew.

Having no comedian to top the bill could give the committee a long-desired chance to sack him as concert secretary.

"Oh fuckety fuck" he mumbled, as though this prayer to the Lord of Obscenity would solve the problem.

"John could do it" said Terry, to everyone's surprise, especially John's.

"He's the funniest guy I know." agreed Alan. "He regularly has our pub in stitches."

Fat Stan actually smiled, with a possible reprieve in sight.

"Would you do it, mate?" asked, nay pleaded, Stan. "No chance" said John.

"It's a hundred quid" said Stan.

"When am I on?"

"Right, you've got some thinking time. Another twenty minutes for the pie break, then fifteen minutes for the bingo, then Sophie the Stripper is on. Her act is unusual and takes longer than standard. Loads of time. And don't let me down."

Stan, Alan, and Terry headed off for pie and peas, leaving John wondering what he'd done, kept company by Sophie who was heaving some odd kit out of a holdall.

She turned out to be splendid company, as you'd expect from someone who was a philosophy undergraduate by day.

"What did he mean about your act being unusual?" asked John.

"I'm the only stripper who does fire eating as part of her routine," answered Sophie, "and not with my mouth."

She turned her holdall around to reveal her stage name, carefully written in a red flame style – Singed Minge.

"Classy" said John.

"Can you really do comedy in front of this lot?" asked the fire eating philosopher.

"We'll soon know" replied John.

As Einstein and Sophie would probably agree, time is relative, and pies and bingo seemed to rattle by in a blur.

Stan, now positively beaming, stood with John in the wings as they peered at the now darkened concert room, adding drama and great theatricality to Sophie's unusual act.

"Don't forget" said John, "tell them that I've never done this before."

"Trust me" said Stan.

Sophie came off to huge and sooty applause, and Stan almost bounded back on to stage to thank her.

"As some of you might have heard," he lied, "Kenny Ricketts has been taken ill and we send him our best. But – I'm delighted to say that, at great expense, we've managed to get hold of one of clubland's best new comedy talents."

John looked over his shoulder to see who was coming on, then realised that he was it.

"Will you please give a huge welcome to the fantastic – John Bremner!"

In the many years since that day, John had tried to analyse what had happened on the stage.

He did know that two key bits of knowledge popped into his head at the same time.

One was the belief of the old music hall comics that you had seven seconds to get an audience on your side – or not. If you got these first few seconds right, they would laugh at everything and anything.

The second key fact was that nobody in front of him liked Fat Stan.

"Evening all" said John, "and congratulations to Stan."

Stan glowed and gave a thumbs-up from the wings. His smile soon departed.

"Yes," said John, "Stan is the only concert secretary in the Guinness Book of Records – as living proof that Snow White and Dopey did have a child."

The place erupted with laughter, and John had to wait for a chance to deliver gag two.

"Just before I came out, I was watching Roy Orbison on TV – what a performer, known as the Big O. And now here I am, introduced by the Little C."

That one didn't just get a huge laugh – it brought a standing ovation.

The material he kept finding at the back of his mind

was unusual for a club audience used to some rough language and sometimes sheer filth.

He was saucy, but clever, and the audience felt as though they were being treated as intelligent and able to think things through without non-stop four letter assistance.

The next twenty-five minutes went like a dream as John went seamlessly from entertaining a pub to absolutely storming one of the hardest audiences anywhere.

He was dripping sweat as he left the stage to huge applause – and he had learned two things. He could do this – and he loved how it felt.

Afterwards at the bar, John was receiving compliment after compliment. Even Stan was enjoying it as he bathed in praise for finding this comedy genius. He even felt like part of it all as he'd been the butt of much of John's routine.

The big stroke of luck was still to come for John.

After biding his time, a man came over, and, just by the way he carried himself, you could tell that he was a bit different from the rest of the crowd.

He turned out to be an accountant, brought along tonight as a "treat" by the club committee as he had just completed the annual audit.

"That was outstanding" he said to John, "Could you speak at our annual dinner? It's on November 9th."

John took out his diary from a damp inside pocket and pretended to concentrate on what was really a week empty of anything.

"Yes, I could do that" said John, thinking of a bit of fun and a free night out somewhere grand.

"The budget's a bit tight" said Accountant Man, "would you do it for seven hundred and fifty?"

Trying hard to look complacent at the mention of a figure which was more than his monthly salary at the office, he nodded "Go on then, as it's you."

And so, the long and winding journey began, like them all, with one step.

CHAPTER 3 – 1992

By a mathematical chance it was exactly ten years after that landmark night in a boozy workies' club that John's gift for having people in the right place at the right time popped up again.

It was also about twenty years before the strange phone call from John's accountant to his wife, but that was a chapter still to come.

By now, John was really clocking up the miles as the big speaking engagements tended to be in the major cities rather than his native north east of England.

Sometimes wife Janet would come along for the trip, but tonight was standard fare speaking to a Civil Engineers' dinner in Birmingham and it was a solo trip.

The routine was familiar, and, for John, it had a crop of attractive qualities.

He was very well looked after for a start. A far cry from that unforgettable broom cupboard, he was provided with a top end room in the hotel hosting the dinner, and a very large fee.

He now had a good agent on his side, but many bookings came along from a night just like this, with several of the attendees keeping an eye for a future speaker for their own dinners.

As well as the Civil Engineers in attendance, many of their clients were there as guests covering a range of other lines of business – lawyers, accountants, bankers, the travel trade – you name it.

The other great thing about a speaking engagement like this one was that the build-up would be ideal. Before John's stint there would be two big cheeses from the

Civil Engineers giving short speeches about the joys of business. On one occasion, the two warm up chaps had droned on about the importance of concrete to the Lithuanian economy; by the time John took to his feet, he could have read the phone book and gone down well.

He didn't really do nerves any more, but he did apprehension and good preparation.

Late afternoon, he found the function room and checked out the microphone and the acoustics of the room. Most decent hotels had a good quality sound system, but it felt better to be sure. He also liked to walk the room and get a feel of the sight lines from the viewpoint of the audience.

Earlier in his career, John had been lucky enough to work alongside the great Bob Monkhouse who was a splendid teacher of the speaker's art.

Bob confirmed that the old musical hall acts reckoned that you had well under a minute to get an audience on your side. If you had them with you, they would laugh at just about anything: if not, the funniest story on the planet could fall flat.

Mr Monkhouse was also a meticulous dresser. Having the best dinner suit in the room was a sign of respect for your audience and did wonders for your confidence too.

This meant a bespoke suit and proper patent leather shoes. A good watch also helped; you didn't have to flash it, but knowing that there was a Rolex on your wrist provided a real lift.

He also had drinking rules which John adopted; nothing before your turn at the mic and only one glass of red wine in front of you during the dinner.

You would take the occasional sip but never let it get

down to the level where the waiter would top it up. That glass of wine was an important stage prop, though, as it showed the audience that you were part of the event and not effectively standing apart from it with only water or orange juice in front of you.

Ever the detail man, Bob specified red rather than white wine to make it easily visible from the far corners of the room.

Taking the time involved in the top table reception and the dinner itself, there would be about three or four hours when the speaker was on show, and a wine drinking stint of that length would leave you incapable – and he had the evidence to prove it.

At one engagement in Edinburgh, the chap next to John on top table broke most rules in the book, including wearing a handed down dinner suit which would have spoiled a scarecrow's image and a pair of dirty shoes which had rarely seen polish.

This guy wasn't a pro speaker, but he was national president of the host association and it might have been nice to look the part – and sound right when he was due to speak just before John topped the bill.

The biggest rule he trashed was drinking like a fish right through the evening. The dinner was sponsored by a local whisky distillery and they had kindly supplied a bottle of splendid malt at each guest's place.

John was looking forward to taking his home and enjoying a dram or two on a night off. The Scottish chap next to him got through most of his during the dinner, along with much wine and beer.

He hadn't taken the visual tip of seeing the main speaker drinking several glasses of water and simply leaving the glass of red wine on show in front of him.

As dessert was cleared and the speeches were imminent, John leaned over to his companion with the increasingly loud behaviour and slurry words.

"Looks like we are both due on soon" said John. "I'm just going to ask the waiter to bring some more water. Can I get some for you too?"

The reply was littered with an impressive range of obscenities as Mr McDrunkard proposed the view that he didn't need a fucking Sassenach to teach him how to drink.

His voice, even without the mic, was loud enough for the nearest dozen tables to hear his thoughts and they decided as one that some good advice was exactly what he required.

"Fair enough" said John and decided that this was not the night for an intellectual debate.

The toastmaster in his striking cherry red jacket called the room to order and introduced their regional chairman, clearly a popular guy in local business circles judging by the warm and welcoming round of applause.

He gave the perfect speech for the occasion. In just under ten minutes he thanked the guests for their wonderful work for the local economy and charities, told them how proud he was to be their chairman and told a gentle gag which went down well. He then told them again how lovely they were and sat down to a very warm response.

The toastmaster also had his doubts about the drunken president due on next who was now adding a range of bodily noises to the evening, clearly not going down well with the female chair of the local Chamber of

Commerce sitting on his other side.

He'd had a ham-fisted go at chatting her up during the dinner and, major surprise, she had not taken up his range of generous offers.

Anyway, the toastmaster did his job and introduced the chap and he received a much lighter round of applause, especially from the tables at the front who'd heard his earlier attempt at the Olympic swearing record.

John's memory of the next twenty seconds would live with him forever.

Trying to look impressive for once, Mr President stood to attention, ramrod straight like a soldier. The sudden rush of blood glazed his eyes and, in a remarkable physical performance, he vomited down his chest and fell forward, still rigid, over top table.

The sound effects were something else too.

In rapid succession, there were the noises of his technicolour yawn, then the crashing of several wine glasses and bottles he'd knocked over, producing a crashing symphony on the polished parquet floor. The climax came with his drunken face smacking into the floor too.

Luckily, a local doctor was seated just in front of him and moved at speed to get him into the recovery position and open his airways. With remarkable efficiency, paramedics were soon at the hotel and wheeled him away covered with a red blanket.

Apparently, he woke up late the next day with little memory of the night before. Sadly, for a man who had taken a business lifetime to rise to the post of national president, the only thing his whole profession would now remember him for was his dramatic performance that night.

The whole episode was soon over, the hubbub subsided and the toastmaster gave the main speaker a very polished introduction. It was bound to be good as John had written it for him; he'd discovered years back that a few sentences outlining your pedigree impressed the audience and got him off to a good start.

John had most of his intended speech in his head but always liked to start with a few lines which were topical and fitted the surroundings.

"Well" said John, "I may not be as acrobatic as your last speaker, but I will be on longer."

That produced the first good laugh of the night, to be followed by many more in the forty minutes or so of wit and wisdom.

This was followed by a very warm ovation and a splendid vote of thanks from the regional chairman, glad to see his big evening saved after the performance by the vomiting clown.

A welcome glass of cognac was soon on the way and John was ready for an important part of the night – effectively his after-dinner sales operation.

Lots of people came up to compliment him on his stint and John made sure that they went away with his business card – many future bookings would come from that.

Even his business card was a work of art – stylish and simple with gold lettering on a polished grey background.

There was an etiquette in these things. This booking had come to John directly after passing on a card at a

Law Society dinner in Leeds, so it was his personal card which he handed over. If it had been a booking fixed by his agent Lucy, it would have been one of hers.

It was important to do things the right way – if you didn't, karma came back to bite you.

It wasn't just one-way traffic though – several of the admiring guests passed on a room number with an invitation to their "after show party."

Several professions did this, but the Civil Engineers were particularly fine in this regard.

The plan was to book a suite and invite a dozen or so of your existing, or potential, clients for an hour or two of drinks and a bit of fun.

This was of a largely innocent variety, usually with something like a golf simulator or a Scalextric race track to get guests relaxed and chatty.

After about twenty minutes of networking, John had ten of these invitations and was determined to get around and visit them all – for courtesy, to add a bit of kudos for the client, and to continue the sowing of business cards to reap future gigs.

After another hour, he was doing well – six of the parties attended, good contacts made and a glow from a few drinks now that his working stint was about done.

The next card on his hit list was showing Suite 464 which looked to be well along the corridor from the party he was just leaving.

What he encountered on the way was far from innocent.

It was a huge hotel and it seemed that some of it was being refurbished, or tarted up, whichever way you looked at it.

Counting off the room numbers, he was certainly going the right way as he headed into what looked like a kind of foyer midway along the corridor. There were a few stepladders leaning against the walls, some dust sheets, and the gloomy look which comes with subdued safety lighting rather than the sparkling chandeliers of the main corridors.

He headed into the cave-like atmosphere and saw the rest of the well-lit corridor ahead and the location of his next mini-party.

Going from mega-brightness to near darkness meant that he could hardly see a thing at first but, as his eyes adjusted, he was aware of some movement to his right. In the centre of the space some fixture had been covered with heavy plastic sheets for protection from the painters.

It could have been anything from a grand piano to a reception desk, but what was happening upon it was of more interest. Bending over the plastic-garlanded structure was a lady in a black cocktail-style dress and her movement was making the plastic sheet squeak in a regular rhythm.

Her dress was up and her pants were down and it was the dinner-suited chap behind her who was keeping the steady beat going. His trousers were down and he was clearly playing "hide the sausage" with some enthusiasm.

Being British, John tried not to continue watching and picked up his pace while concentrating on counting his own shoes, as you do in such circumstances.

This was the second display of physical jerks that John had seen in the evening and the male half of this one won John's eternal admiration. Without missing a beat, he combined a big smile with a shout of "Excellent speech, sir!"

The lady didn't comment, so perhaps she didn't like it.

John couldn't help wondering whether he should hold up score cards for style and technique as in ice skating.

A few seconds later, John was at his latest party and wondering to himself if he'd really seen what he'd just witnessed – he had.

He completed his rounds, gave thanks to his host and wandered back to his own room, to have the ultimate relaxation of throwing off his formal wear and flopping onto the huge bed.

He knew he wouldn't sleep for a while. After a speech, it was like coming off stage and he would take a while to come down. The after-show drinks had helped but he knew that a racing mind would keep him awake.

He was pondering the two drunken cabarets of earlier and wondered about writing a book entitled "Things We Do When Pissed."

His mind went back to a dinner he'd performed at in Belfast when the speaker before him was the coach of the Irish Rugby side. He was a mountain of a man, and like tonight's character, he had drunk far too much. His sheer size meant that the alcohol took a while to affect his faculties, but the full effect switched on as he spoke.

He had a broad accent, slurred his words, and was far too close to the mic. The result was that a stream of gibberish came out at a sound level which would have been a bit over the top for Wembley Stadium.

The audience was very polite for about thirty seconds but then started to chat among themselves in the absence of much else to do.

Mr Man Mountain heard the chatter and realised that they were ignoring him. For the only time in the evening, his voice became slow, clear and distinct as he described in chilling detail what would happen to the next guy who spoke when he was on.

He then went back to deafening garbage, accompanied by the surreal sight of several hundred dinner-suited guests listening in silence to his non-words.

At the end of one verbal torrent, he paused, looked at what he could see of the audience and then at John sitting next to him, who guessed that this was probably at the point of a punch line in what he thought was a highlight in his stunning delivery.

Wanting to survive the night, John laughed like a drain and slapped his thighs, with the rest of the traumatised audience following suit.

This pattern of noise, pause and laughter went on for a while until John had an internal panic at the thought of another possibility. What if one incomprehensible burst was really him saying "And then my whole family was killed in the plane crash" – and John led a huge roar of laughter.

Happily, the problem never arose because, half way through another torrent of noise, the rugby chap groaned and collapsed in a heap on the floor.

With that happy memory in mind, sleep eventually came to John and he was out like a light until eight the next morning – happy and a few grand richer.

CHAPTER 4 – 1992 – THE NEXT MORNING

The next day started for John with, if it's even possible, multiple smiles on his face.

The first came from waking up in his peaceful room, Daily Telegraph under the door, and the prospect of a leisurely Saturday morning breakfast and a few wake-up coffees before he drove home.

Another part of his wake-up ritual was to get out for a walk – partly to clear the head and because, if you didn't, all you saw was the hotel.

In a city centre, a bit of shopping and a little gift to take home would be on the agenda, but this hotel was almost in the countryside, next to the National Exhibition Centre, so semi-rural delights awaited.

From his window, John could see a sunlight-dappled lake with some friendly looking ducks. A cup of coffee there would be just the job.

Sometimes the Saturday morning walk would produce a great comedy moment. One Saturday, John woke up in Goole, not far from Hull, after speaking to the Institute of Freight Forwarders.

After breakfast he asked the girl on reception if he needed a taxi into the town centre or would it be walkable.

"No problem" was the advice, "Turn left out of the hotel and it's five minutes' walk, tops."

After walking for longer than that, John wondered if there was a turning he should have taken.

A cloth capped local was walking towards him and so he asked for directions to the elusive town centre.

"You're in it, cocky bugger" came the welcoming reply.

Perhaps four charity shops and a Boots the Chemist did constitute a major urban centre after all.

Because it was Saturday, the phone wouldn't ring much, but John was becoming aware of the necessity of staying in touch.

Feeling very high-tech, he had his very first mobile phone and following generations would find it a great source of laughter and bemusement.

It was literally the size of a brick, weighed about the same, and did a fraction of the jobs the later smartphones would do. John lugged his about in a special case, but some friends had brought shoulder holsters which they thought made them look very trendy – they were wrong.

Youngsters in the 21st Century wouldn't believe how primitive these phones were – no memory, no answerphone, and very dodgy reception unless you were very lucky.

John was very up with the times though in having his new mobile number on his business cards and it was starting to bear fruit.

Most people waited for business calls until Monday, but his mobile rang twice in a matter of minutes while he was grappling with the devilish Saturday Telegraph cryptic crossword clue and a very strong coffee.

He recognised the voice of the first caller as an American in the property business who had hosted one of last night's after-show affairs, and he remembered that he had been very complimentary.

"Morning John" he launched in, "you were great last night and I'd love you to speak at my real estate conference."

"Could you block out a few days and it would be great if you could host our awards ceremony and a Q&A too?"

The proposed dates were clear and what came up next proved the point of John being in the right place last night.

"Look" said Mr American, "I'm asking for three days of your time, but I'll add a week's holiday if you can.

Bring your wife and you can chill out in the penthouse suite at one of our hotels."

One of our hotels? This sounded good.

"Would ten thousand dollars, the hotel and business class flights work for you?"

Business class – from Newcastle?

"I can go with that" said John, "but I forgot to ask – where is your conference?"

"Sorry, should have said, it's Las Vegas if that's ok for you."

It certainly was. A promise to have a confirmation sent over on Monday. No, not sent, couriered, and they could do lunch next time Mr America was at his London club to talk it through.

This was a bloody long way from doing a turn in a workies' club.

He was just about to ring home with the good news, when the brick ring again.

John had a flair for recognising voices and this one was easy to recall from another after-show party the night before: an accent he couldn't place, a hell of a suntan and an air of quiet affluence.

It felt like waking up on in the millionaires' club. This

guy probably out-trumped the American – he was massively complimentary and outlined his business interests which included owning a hotel in Corfu – and cruise ships. As you do.

A few dates checked, a bit of minor haggling, and John's diary now included speaking at the beautiful Marbella Corfu, holiday included, and a series of cruise ships.

The day couldn't get any better – and then it did.

The phone rang in the room and it was going to be either John's wife or his agent – the two people he gave contact details to as a matter of routine in case the brick ran out of juice or range.

It was agent Lucy who had a speaking query for a lovely hotel which John knew well – Mottram Hall in Cheshire, land of the local gentry and over-paid footballers.

Somebody up there was clearly rooting for John, and coffee with the ducks before the drive home tasted even better.

CHAPTER 5 – AUTUMN 1992 – AUCTIONS AND HECKLERS

After that lovely morning of fine phone calls near Birmingham, one of John's regular treats was looking at his diary for the good things in store. As well as a useful crop of UK gigs to come, the future joys of Las Vegas, Corfu and cruise ships were on the horizon.

The next English biggie was the hosting of a testimonial dinner in London. This was a benefit event for the brilliant West Indies fast bowler Courtney Walsh and many of cricket's big names would be there.

In the days before telephone number salaries in professional sport, the benefit year was a great way for fans to pay tribute to a great in cricket or football and give him a nest egg for a happy life after sport.

Compering an event and running the required auction was much harder that it looked. Part of the skill was making it look as if anyone could do it – they couldn't.

John had acquired a top-notch reputation for his ability to get the job done properly and, as well as the usual speaker's list of learned rules, there were a few extra points to remember. It was essential to keep the pace of the night going and time the auction to get maximum income from the audience. This was a finely tuned operation to get maximum earnings from the auction – too early and they were too sober to be generous, too late and they were too ratted to care. Hit the sweet spot and all would be well.

There was also some homework to be done in checking who the potential big spenders at the dinner would be – and what would massage their sizeable egos.

There were a few potential hazards to recognise too – including the curse, and the blessing, of the heckler.

A witty heckle was a good chance for John to respond with his skills of repartee – a drunk who was too far gone was a waste of time.

Many people thought that there was no such thing as an ad lib which came out of nowhere and that was largely true. Instead, a top speaker had a huge library of responses in his head and the trick was to use one at the perfect time.

One of John's favourite memories of just such a triumph at a dinner in Cambridge. A sharp-witted heckler had engaged with John, and the audience loved the experience of enjoying a volley of repartee played at the pace of top class tennis.

The guy had been through a bottle of decent wine or two and was just enough within the world of the living to keep up with John. As always when speaking, John was sober and stayed on top when the heckler finally succumbed to alcohol.

The Wimbledon atmosphere continued as almost a thousand people swivelled heads from side to side to watch the top-level contest.

Coming to a head, the heckler rose to his feet to deliver what he thought would be the killer line.

As with Mr McDrunkard in Edinburgh, it was the sudden rush of blood to the head which was the problem.

The overpowering dizziness and tilt forward meant that he instinctively tried to grab the table for support. He almost made it but grabbed the white tablecloth instead and took it, and everything on it, to the polished floor with him.

This included several wine bottles and the huge array of plates and glasses which the ten guests around the table had used over the last few hours.

The brave heckler was looking peacefully asleep in the middle of the debris, and with a theatricality not possessed by all crockery, the last plate gave a brilliant drum roll before all ended in silence.

A thousand pairs of eyes swivelled to see how John would respond and he did – brilliantly.

"There you go" he said, "you see what happens when cousins marry."

Everyone in the room, bar one, joined in a standing ovation.

A contented John knew that the line had been used a time or two before, but rarely as well as that.

He would be a lucky man if such a chance came up at tonight's cricketing dinner, but careful preparation would mean that all would go well.

The dinner was being held at the flagship Hilton in Park Lane and, as all its rooms were booked, John and the top table contingent had been booked in at the Grosvenor House Hotel just along the road.

John had completed his afternoon check of the room and the sound system and gone back to the hotel to relax for a while before changing into his working wear of dinner suit.

Then he was back to the Hilton to make last minute checks before the guests began to arrive.

The huge ballroom looked superb, with huge cricket photos and memorabilia on the walls, along with colourful Caribbean posters promoting the evening's sponsors Mount Gay Rum and Red Stripe Lager, two great tastes of sunshine.

Also arriving early was West Indian cricket legend Clive Lloyd who would be paying tribute to beneficiary Courtney during the evening.

John had worked alongside the great man before and was greeted with a huge smile and handshake of recognition.

He leant in towards John and said in tones of liquid gold, "Don't forget John. Lots of lovely rum cocktails; just one each for me and you till later."

He had the same professional approach as John and it worked – by nine 'o'clock that evening, they were the only two in the room who knew whether they were Arthur or Martha.

The evening flowed, as planned, like a well-oiled machine. Film of Courtney flattening cricket stumps around the world, a bouncy two-way with John, and fulsome words of tribute from Clive.

A short comfort break was called and then the fund-raising could begin.

Benefit organiser Phil shook John's hand. "Well done mate, brilliantly set up. I have a dream of you making ten grand on the auction tonight."

For an expert in these things, it turned out that he was way off with his target.

The auction lots were a good mixture; Caribbean holidays and cricket matches with a good face value, and bats and shirts which were cheap yet priceless because of the signatures of the top names.

In those days before collapsing banks and corporate prudence were heard of, there were ripe pickings for a good auctioneer and John was the best.

A mixture of fun and top audience management soon had the money rolling in. John knew the big business faces in the room and exactly how to milk them in a nice way.

One of the biggest successes was an engineered bidding battle for dinner with Courtney and a signed shirt with photos of the occasion – face value of about £250.

John had the bid up to an amazing fifteen grand with Simon of Global Invest ahead of arch friendly rival James of Eastland Bank.

"Well" said John, "it looks like the star prize is going to Simon Oliver of Global Invest, the most generous man in British business, unless someone knows better?"

He swivelled his gaze to James who took the bait and brought a huge round of applause with his new winning bid of twenty grand. The days had not yet come when shareholders might look a bit quizzically at such spending, but James considered it money well spent for his place in business legend.

The money racked up at a record pace with big days out at famous cricket grounds like Lord's on the menu, and then John decided to play his wild card.

Despite being a regular guest at some top-level football grounds, John still had massive affection for his little home town club of Hartlepool United.

A phone call to a friend at the club had brought forth a hospitality box for a home game at one of their lower league fixtures.

John caught the mood and the goodwill perfectly as he announced, "And now the crown jewels – a hospitality box for ten and a chance to meet the players at – wait for it – Hartlepool United."

A huge wave of laughter, and a round of applause, showed that John had them with him. Five minutes later, he had added another five grand to the pot, having sold something which could have been had for about £200 with one phone call.

There had been some fine audience humour during the battle for a day out in Hartlepool on the north-east coast of England, and John decided to really go for it.

"Right" he said, "Some of you have almost suggested that a trip to my home town is not on your bucket list.

I know we started to worry when we head that Ethiopia were holding rock concerts for us, but we are lovely really.

Who'll give me £500 not to go to Hartlepool?"

A huge roar of laughter was followed by a crazy bidding battle, and, as would be recounted a thousand times by everyone present, £3,500 was soon in the pot for the world's most unlikely auction lot.

John's skill in keeping the night moving meant that there was time to enjoy at the end of the evening for good company and the sheer joy which made such events memorable.

Organiser Phil, beneficiary Courtney and star man Clive advanced on John as one and gave him a joint bear hug and a resulting photo which would take a cherished spot in his growing collection.

With a huge smile, Phil announced that John's auction had shot over the ten-grand target and had clocked an unbelievable £73,000.

"As soon as we are done and dusted here" beamed Phil, "top table back to the hotel and thank-you drinks on me."

Not long afterwards, a very happy band strolled through a warm night in Park Lane and were soon supremely comfortable in rich red leather chairs in a bar which reeked of luxury.

Phil, still purring, called over the waiter and gave concise instructions. "Don't take a penny from these guys. Put it all on room 232 and let's start with some champagne."

John spent more time listening than talking, and glowed in new friendships and Caribbean cricket.

After a fine flow of champagne, rum cocktails and cognac, it was way into the early hours when Courtney drew himself to his considerable height and announced that he was off to bed.

"I'm on breakfast television tomorrow" he said "and I'd better be awake. Thanks everybody and especially you John – you're a star!"

This was perfect, but then came a snag.

Courtney headed over to reception for his room key and, after some discussion, it seemed that the hotel had no record of him being checked in.

Clive Lloyd followed, with the same result.

John remembered, just, changing into his dinner suit not that long ago, so they must have his key.

No, they didn't.

Phil was beyond mildly annoyed by now and said to the young receptionist with some feeling, "We've just had a superb night and your hotel has given it a poor ending."

"For Grosvenor House, this is a disgrace."

With a melting smile, the receptionist paused before replying.

"I can't speak for Grosvenor House sir, but this is the Dorchester."

The red-faced band stumbled down Park Lane to where they should be, with the silence broken by Phil's parting thought.

"The poor bugger in 232 is going to get a shock when he sees his check-out bill."

He went back the next day to settle up. He said.

CHAPTER 6 – FREEBIES AND COUNTRY CLUBS

Like most people, John had had close contact with some of the bad news of everyday life including friends and family who had been victims of the nightmares of cancer and other serious problems out of the blue.

For many great causes which raised funds to fight back against these curses of modern life, he was always happy to speak or compere an event as a freebie. He'd soon learned the big difference in wanting to donate his time and skills for free and the people who thought they could demand it as a right.

With musician friends and other creative types, he would often compare notes on the wide range of cheeky requests and the range of polite responses in dealing with them.

A call would sometimes come claiming that there was no fee available, but the appearance would be a "terrific shop window".

John often felt like pointing out that he had been a professional speaker for some considerable time now and people had enjoyed many chances to go window shopping and make up their minds about booking him or not.

Instead, he found it worked well to turn the conversation around to the business of the caller.

On one occasion, he discovered that the enquirer ran a chain of top end jewellery shops.

Bingo.

"Perfect" said John, "my wife's been after a really expensive diamond necklace for a while, and if you provide one for free, it will be a great shop window!"

Job done.

The daftest thing was that the biggest freebie hunters were the ones who could most afford to pay the going rate.

One of the best came one afternoon and the caller had a typical over-egged plummy voice – always an early warning sign.

"Good to talk to you" began the caller, "I saw you speak at the accountants' dinner in Bristol recently and thought you were jolly super. I'm President of the Institute of Bankers in the north west of England next year and wondered if you were free to speak at my dinner."

John checked and was happy to say that the proposed date was free.

"Splendid" said Mr Plummy, "let me have the best address for you and I'll drop you a line to confirm."

Half expecting this, John dived straight back, "What kind of budget are you working on?"

"In what sense old chap?"

"In the sense of my fee; I'm a professional speaker."

"Oh – we don't normally pay a fee to our speakers."

"Who did it last year?" enquired John and discovered it was the local vicar who was a friend of the organiser.

"And did he go down well?"

"Oh, no, he was a shambles."

"Ask him again" suggested John who was now half enjoying the banter.

"I don't know how we are going to sort this one" pondered Mr Plummy.

With a flash of inspiration, John did.

He had no current plans to move house, but invented

a situation where he did.

"I presume you are a banker yourself" asked John.

"Oh yes, in charge of one of the biggest in Manchester, don't you know?"

"Perfect" said John. "We are hoping to move house soon" he lied, "but the market is slow and we are going to need a bridging loan of about a million for a year or so. If you could do that at no cost, I'll do your dinner for free."

"We'd soon go out of business doing that" bristled an outflanked Mr Plummy.

"Me too" said John before wishing him well in his speaker search and hanging up.

John enjoyed fighting his corner and keeping a sense of his own value when necessary.

By contrast, his next engagement was a freebie he was happy to do and close to home; a fund-raising dinner for a breast cancer charity at the Roker Country Club just up the road, between Sunderland and Newcastle.

The "country club" description always made John crease with internal laughter. This place was a cheap and cheerful dump and it only stayed in business because, at about 650 capacity, it had one of the biggest function rooms in the patch.

John had spoken at some very swish spots throughout the country which really deserved the name, but he had also survived some amazing dives which must have staggered guests who thought they were heading for somewhere at the top of the pile.

One of the classics was just outside Manchester and memories of the place still made John and his wife quiver with laughter.

John had been speaking at the Chamber of Commerce Dinner at the excellent SAS Radisson Hotel on the Manchester Airport site and, for reasons he never discovered other than comedy potential, they had accommodation reserved for him at the Didsbury Country House Hotel not too far away.

Janet had come along for the trip so that they could visit her family in Yorkshire on the way home. She was not attending the Chamber Dinner, but ate at the "country house" before getting her feet up with the TV and a bottle of wine in the room.

This place was in the low-end category – room, food and service were distinctly average and the whole place looked as if it had been last decorated just after the war.

John's performance at the dinner went down a storm and he enjoyed the usual post-match networking and sowing of business cards before his hosts organised a car back to his room for the night.

The couple of hours after doing an after-dinner was like coming off stage – especially after a successful stint, you were as high as a kite and unlikely to sleep for a few hours.

John was soon back at the hotel and was expecting a nightcap in a sleepy bar, but, to his surprise, he could hear sounds of major jollity coming from the corridor beyond the reception desk.

An enquiry to the desk chap brought the welcome news that the "cabaret club" was on until two. He bounded upstairs and found Janet still awake with the wine nearly gone.

"Great news" he said, "the dinner went like a dream and there's a night club downstairs – throw something on and we'll take a look."

And so, with John still in his DJ and Janet in a sparkly top she always brought "just in case", they ventured towards the source of the noise.

Even before they got into the bar proper, the first sight they saw would live with them forever.

Leaning on the bar in an elegant white tuxedo was a chap who looked like a retired colonel with his lady in a floor length evening dress.

They had clearly been conned by the "country house" tag too.

They were both standing in a state of shock with mouths hanging open. John guessed that they were staying over before taking an early morning flight to an exotic destination.

The guy who had turned them into statues was a blue comedian who would make late night entertainment in the back streets of Amsterdam or Hamburg look tame.

With a herd of local ladies lapping it up, he was conducting a quiz game which would probably never make it to mainstream television.

It was called – *Show us your fanny for a can of lager*.

The way things were going, John wondered if it would be on Saturday night TV one day – but not yet.

Like the retired colonel and his wife, John and Janet stood transfixed as though they had crossed the boundary into a parallel universe.

John had that night very much in his head as he drove up the A19 for his fund-raising stint at another of the country house family which had clear similarities to its Manchester relative.

John's usual check of the function room showed that, despite the obvious deficiencies in the venue, it should work ok. The room looked pleasant enough despite the badly dated pine cladding on the walls which was parting company with the plaster in places.

Tickets had obviously sold well, and John worked out that they had jammed just over 700 places into the space for 600 – getting between the tables would be a battle for guests and staff alike.

On the positive side, the dinner was receiving considerable support from Wear Freight, a well-respected locally based shipping company.

John knew their Chairman, Bob, one of the region's nice guys. His mother had been through breast cancer and his name behind the event had helped to produce the sell-out.

Bob was also using the night to entertain some of his business contacts, including a batch from overseas. It was always funny to hear politicians singing the praises of international trade as though it were a new idea.

Companies like Wear Freight, and many others, had enjoyed a good trading relationship with a wide range of international partners for many years, and had adapted as the world had changed.

At one time, huge quantities of timber came from Scandinavia to supply pit props for the region's coal mines. The introduction of metal hydraulic props, followed by the closure of the pits, had dented that market, but other goods had taken their place, from consumer goods to cars.

It wasn't just business connections either; firm friendships had developed and a look through north east phone books showed a range of Scandinavian family names. Proof indeed that the early Viking invasions had been replaced by more subtle courtship.

On this particular evening, Bob had one particular guest in his sights; Sven Christiansen, the boss of Gothenburg Metals – a huge potential partner.

Wear Freight had really pushed the boat out. A good friend owned the regional Volvo dealership and had kindly agreed to pick up the Swedish guest personally and attend the dinner too.

This was an impressive pick-up at Newcastle Airport; not any old taxi but a new top of the range Volvo saloon driven by the MD who had a decent smattering of Swedish too.

He was delivered to the hotel and had been welcomed with wine in his room before the dinner. Chairman Bob knew that, with John's expert help, Sven would be made to feel like a VIP and would be well on the way to signing a key contract.

Bob's only little worry was that the hotel would struggle to fit the VIP role as well as he would have wished.

As always, the "country house" showed a remarkable lack of business sense in making the most of what should have been the gold mine of 700 people wanting to spend their money and have a good time.

The bar was heaving by 7'o'clock and the two young bar staff were struggling to cope.

Regulars knew that the Duke of York pub just over the road was the spot to head for in the expectation of being served quickly.

They were well known for keeping an eye on the

dinners diary at the hotel over the road and putting a dozen bar staff on between seven and eight before the function began.

The usual result was that the pub took well over five grand in that hour and the hotel took peanuts.

Chairman Bob, John and the top table guests didn't have that problem as they were in the VIP reception in the suite above the function room, but a glance out of the window told them that normal pub service was going well.

A swarm of dinner-suited guests were holding up the traffic as they crossed the road carrying huge quantities of drinks.

Eventually, the room was full, the pub had gone quiet, and John began his introductions to the audience with maximum reputation enhancement.

He drew a standing ovation for Chairman Bob in recognition of his charity work and an equally warm welcome for "our most welcome guest Sven – Swedish by birth but an adopted north-easterner."

Even better, John had discovered during reception drinks that Sven was a big charity supporter in Sweden, and had a particular affection for breast cancer charities which had helped two members of his own family.

A quiet discussion had produced a plan which John could now reveal to the audience.

As the applause for the Swedish visitor still hung in the air, John fixed his gaze on the far end of the room and said, "Ladies and gentlemen, just listen to this – I've never seen anything like this in my life."

John had to wait only seconds for total silence and then continued;

"I've had the pleasure of chatting to Sven earlier this evening, and introducing him to our friends from Breast Cancer North East. He must have been very impressed."

"Will you please welcome to the microphone, Sally Johnson, Chief Exec of that lovely charity which does such wonderful work in our patch."

Sally took a while to wriggle between the crammed-in tables and reached John who put a friendly arm around her shoulder and squeezed her nervousness away.

"We're going to have a great night for your charity Sally, and how about this for a kick-off. With a flourish, he produced a piece of paper from his inside pocket like a magician revealing a rabbit.

"Sally, courtesy of Bob's special guest Sven and Gothenburg Metals, I am delighted to present this cheque for" – and he spread the words perfectly – "TWENTY FIVE THOUSAND POUNDS."

The place erupted and a tearful Sally produced the perfect picture for the business magazine photographer as she hugged Sven and Bob.

Courtesy of John's skilful diplomacy, the charity had received a windfall, Sven was now a star in the region, and Bob thought that this was simply a wonderful piece of relationship building which nothing could spoil.

He'd forgotten which hotel they were in.

Jamming too many tables into the room showed a commercial appetite which wasn't matched by their pre-event staffing ratio, but they had a kind of solution for the human log jam.

All the waitresses looked like a cross between rugby players and brick out-dwellings and simply ploughed between tables like human battering rams.

On top table, John was watching Bob and Sven getting along famously, with Sven glowing after his generosity and numerous warm compliments.

He really looked the part – a cross between a Viking and a king of the boardroom. His brushed back blond hair and his golden beard set off what was clearly a very expensive dinner suit – beautiful cloth, silk lapels and, as John knew well, made to measure by a good tailor.

Sadly, those silk lapels and a bulldozing waitress would soon meet.

The hotel didn't go in for elegant sauces or elegant anything.

The technique was for each waitress to carry two enormous jugs of hot gravy which were poured on the guests' dinner plates like a jobbing gardener watering the plants at high speed.

Trying to slow down too late, one of the waitresses crashed into the top table guests and launched forward.

With supreme slapstick skill she poured a full jug of gravy down the left lapel of Sven's expensive suit.

"Friggin' arseholes" she apologised, and yanked a grimy tea towel from her waistband. She used it to grind the gravy into the silk and looked pleased with her efforts.

To his credit, Sven laughed as Big Bertha went off to create more mayhem elsewhere.

Things ticked over well until the sweet course which, by hotel standards, was ambitious – apple pie and custard.

The gravy jugs had been rinsed, probably, and were now filled with custard and being delivered by the same determined waitresses.

The dropped jug of hot custard could have landed on one of 700 people, but, of course, it landed on Sven. It was a different waitress and the other lapel, but the language and the tea towel cure were identical.

Bob was starting to worry – would this be the first major contract in business history to be scuppered by a double assault of gravy and custard.

Sven, well lubricated, was still taking it well when another of the hotel's serving techniques marked it out as not being of the Mayfair School.

The waitresses' biceps were being further tested as they carried huge pre-ordered jugs of beer and lager to the tables.

As one of the Amazons passed top table, Sven grabbed her beer jug and announced, "before you do dear" and tipped it over his own head.

Bob didn't know whether to laugh or cry.

Considering the triple food and beverage assault, the night went well and ended with nightcaps with the key guests.

A lot of malt whisky, Sven's favourite, was consumed and he went off to bed smiling rather than frowning.

The next morning, Bob and John heard what had happened next.

Sven had entered his room and discovered it to be far too warm – partly because of his boozy night, and also because of the hotel's ancient heating system which tended to be cold or hot, but nothing in between.

He had been given the best room in the hotel, which wasn't saying much, but at least it had two doors leading on to a balcony.

He opened them wide and stepped out to take a welcome blast of air. Directly beneath him, he could see the lovely new shiny Volvo which had brought him here.

He was about to lean on the balcony rail and thought better of it; its rust would probably further damage his suit and a few missing struts were a cause for concern too.

Leaving the doors open, he went back into the room and peeled off his finery. He wondered if a dry cleaner would be able to rescue the splattered dinner suit or whether it would be a write-off.

Either way, he was a tidy man and hung it on a coat hanger to air off.

The wardrobe had clearly seen better days and the weight of a three-piece suit on the hanging rail ended its life.

The next few seconds reminded John of his childhood visits to the circus when the clowns would bring the house down with their exploding jalopy of a car which dropped to pieces.

The dinner suit caused the hanging rail to drop to the floor of the rickety wardrobe, but that was only the start of it.

The roof of the wardrobe crashed down to the floor too, the back collapsed against the wall, and the right-hand side panel crashed sideways and produced a theatrical clang against the hot radiator.

All this activity made the left-hand panel spin and fall sideways and backwards, through the open balcony doors. Its progress was halted by the crumbling rail which snapped in half.

One half stayed attached to the balcony floor while the other half, consisting of a long strut with some uprights attached, headed at some speed towards the ground.

It never reached the tarmac as its trajectory was interrupted - by a nice shiny Volvo.

The long metal strut went through the car roof like a huge lance, with the attached uprights shaking like the flights of an arrow.

The next morning, Bob heard the tale from his car dealer friend who assured him that the wrecked car could be sorted on insurance and he'd organise a replacement vehicle to take Sven to Bob's office for lunch – and to sign the contract.

Poor Bob was wondering if that meeting would still happen when his phone rang.

Sven's first words were kind of what he was expecting.

"I've never had a night like that in my life" said Sven.

That seemed true enough, but the next bit was unexpected.

"You are a genius and a friend for life. I could understand you doing your homework and discovering that I'm a massive fan of your wonderful Fawlty Towers – but how on earth did you fix all that business up? "

"It was perfect – the stunt waitresses, the suicidal wardrobe and the railing into the car roof. Sheer class from start to finish."

An hour later, Sven was still laughing as they clinked glasses over the signed contract, one of the biggest ever for Bob's company.

A few months later, the hospitality was returned at a dinner in Gothenburg. Highlights of the trip included Bob's car from the airport landing in the dock, an exploding hotel room, and a night porter who attacked him with an axe.

Sven had clearly become a fan of Psycho as well as Fawlty Towers, and the successful business relationship would be embroidered over the years with an escalation of practical jokes which could only really climax with a nuclear attack.

CHAPTER 7 – CRUISE CAPERS

As well as his considerable mileage around the UK, John was now a firm favourite on cruise ships after that chance meeting with the Greek expert.

Like many things in the speaker business, the more you did, the more you did, and he was enjoying as many cruise ships as he fancied each year.

They looked after him well and Janet usually came along as his guest to see more of the world than they would have dreamt of – and all down to that chance performance in the workies' club all those years before.

The sheer size of the cruise business surprised most people with almost two million Brits a year taking a cruise – and an estimated two thousand speakers at sea at any time.

When you looked at the packages on offer, it was no surprise at all that cruising appealed to so many people.

For many of the older generation especially it had great advantages in economies, convenience, and safety.

A market had developed where many British retired people had taken the option of spending much of the winter at sea.

You could get the kids to house-sit, save on the household bills and shopping, and enjoy some sunshine and relaxation. You'd have your comfy cabin cleaned twice a day and be served good quality meals on a regular basis.

John was a reasonably healthy eater, and he always marvelled at the quantities some guests could get through.

A substantial breakfast would be followed by a big

lunch, then afternoon tea, before a five-course dinner in the evening. For those still feeling hunger pangs, there was the midnight feast and punctuations of gala buffets.

Bar prices were reasonable too, and many passengers supplemented this with their own mini-bar in the cabin, brought from home.

For older people who were time rich, another trend was growing strongly.

If you had family in Australia or New Zealand, you could take a few weeks cruising there from the UK rather than go through the queues and frustrations of a modern airport.

There were no weight restrictions on luggage to worry about, and instead of being wedged in an economy seat for twenty-four hours, you could sleep in a proper bed at night.

You could then stay with the offspring, get to know the grandkids, and set off home eventually on another cruise ship.

It was the safety angle which was a magnet to many people.

Once you had a few decades under your belt, a British town centre at night felt more like a threat than a pleasure. Rowdy idiots who were drunk or drugged and pubs where you couldn't hear yourself think weren't attractive any more.

Many cruise ships had cleverly made themselves feel like town centres but pleasant and safe.

You had a choice of several bars, from those with the feel of a swish club to places which felt like how a pub used to be. You could then dine formally or cheap and cheerful, followed by entertainment which was to your taste – from easy listening vocalists to theatre shows of a fair quality.

Best of all, when the eyes started to droop, there was no over-priced taxi or boozy bus or tube to worry about – a few minutes' stroll and you were back in your cabin.

Even the travelling was easy. One of John's favourite cruises was around the Baltic – fourteen nights calling at some lovely spots in Scandinavia, Estonia, Germany and Russia – and you only unpacked once.

For a speaker, getting it right on a cruise was crucial, and it fitted John's style perfectly; he could be informative and enlightening about the regions the ship visited, but always remembered that people were on holiday and wanted some fun too.

This didn't always happen and it took John a while to work out why someone who was like your worst nightmare of a dull teacher from school made it onto a ship.

As well as Lucy, his regular agent, John had been adopted by Peel Talent, a specialist cruise agency who were careful to vet people they promoted to cruise lines.

They did their research, checked testimonials, and liked to see a show reel.

One or two "agencies" took on anybody who would pay a couple of hundred quid a year to be on their books, but the cruise bookers usually found them out before too long.

Many of those hopeful amateurs were out of their depth and soon found a professional theatre on a cruise ship a very different experience to the local groups where they had volunteered to speak to a tiny audience.

Theatres at sea were often huge, seating around a

thousand, and had top class technical facilities.

The tech operators were outstanding too – often from the Philippines for some reason – and quick to spot what worked – and what didn't.

John had developed friendships with many of these guys and they saw enough speakers on stage to separate the wheat from the chaff.

On one cruise, a female speaker who had clearly slipped through the net achieved a new record in losing an audience quickly.

Word about a speaker spread like wildfire on a cruise ship and John was proud of hitting full houses on a regular basis.

This woman hit a new record in her first three appearances – recording attendances of three hundred, followed by fifty, followed by four – so her final "talk" took place not in the theatre but around a table in the bar.

When John went in to set up for his third talk of the cruise, a full house awaited and techie Alfie greeted him with a big smile and an arm around the shoulder.

"Thank the Lord for you mate" he said. "I've been doing this for nearly ten years now, and you are the best."

Before John could plead modesty and thanks, Alfie returned to his theme.

"That bloody woman" he said "Who let her in front of an audience? She was boring crap."

"You'll have to learn to say what you think Alfie" said John, producing another huge smile.

John enjoyed the buzz of full houses and accepted

that he was never completely off duty. He had a regular queue of passengers eager to chat after every talk, and they'd often stop him to pay a compliment around the ship.

The funny thing about cruises was the Marmite effect – people loved them or hated them – and some people who had never set foot on a ship were experts.

On one occasion, John and Janet had bumped into an old friend at Darlington railway station en route to joining a ship in Southampton.

Telling him where they were headed, he replied "I hate cruise ships."

"What was the last ship you were on?" asked John.

"Oh, I've never been on one." came the baffling reply.

Having said that, some people on board the ships didn't understand them too well either.

Some of the complaints on board were beyond parody, including the fact that the Caribbean was too hot and Alaska was too cold.

The staff on the reception desk were chosen for their ability to stay calm and smile at the occasional passenger who really deserved a good punch.

One classic came from a woman who had been on board for under ten minutes.

She saw her cabin and was soon at reception thumping the desk an hour before the ship was due to sail.

"I paid extra for a sea view cabin" she stormed, "and all I can see are the docks!"

With the smile of an angel, the receptionist replied, "Give it an hour madam."

The crew wondered for a while whether the lady imagined that the quayside was coming with them.

Many of the questions asked on board had passed into legend and were so bizarre that you didn't have to make them up.

For one cruise, John and Janet had been flown out to Mauritius to join a ship on a leg of a world cruise to Cape Town.

One evening, a ship's officer beckoned John over and, speaking in hushed tones, said "I've had two absolute crackers today."

Bearing in mind that the ship was in the middle of the Indian Ocean and three days away from land in either direction, they were a bit special.

The first was a query about whether the crew went home at night.

"Oh yes" replied the officer staying deadpan, "don't you hear the helicopters around midnight?"

It was topped by a passenger asking if the ship made its own electricity.

"Oh no madam, if you notice the map on the television in your cabin, you'll see that we are travelling in a straight line so as not to kink the extension cable which stretches back to Mauritius."

John had seen the weird logic of some passengers at very close quarters, especially on one Caribbean cruise.

As the ship travels west, the passengers are asked to adjust their clocks and watches by an hour on a few occasions so that, when they dock in the West Indies, they are on correct local time.

One morning, John was speaking at eleven, and, as

always afterwards, was enjoying chatting to some passengers who were asking questions or telling their own funny stories.

It was almost noon by the time he was clear and Janet tapped him on the shoulder.

"There's a guy sitting at the front who keeps drumming his fingers on the table and looking daggers at you.

John walked over, smiled and said, "Can I help at all?"

"You can – I'm waiting for your talk to start; it should be on by now!"

"I've just done it" said John.

A collector's item of an answer came back.

"No, you haven't."

It was said with such certainty that John was having doubts himself.

"I promise I have; that's what I was chatting to the passengers about."

A light bulb went on in John's head and he leaned forward to check the irate passenger's watch which did indeed show just after eleven.

"There's the answer" said John. "You should have had a card on your pillow last night about changing the time. It's just after twelve noon ship's time now."

"Oh, I got the card" he said, but I was going to do it tomorrow."

It doesn't work like that.

Word of apology from the passenger came there none; no "silly me" or anything like that. He just wandered off, muttering that it was all the speaker's fault.

John always admired the skills of the masters of the ships; not just the seamanship, but the people management and the view that any problem could be solved.

On that cruise leg, beginning at Mauritius, the first stop was at Reunion Island.

This place always intrigued John; despite being in the Indian Ocean, it was still technically part of France and therefore of the European Union.

Many miles west, in the Atlantic Ocean, lay the Azores, part of Portugal and the EU.

John loved to learn, and to share ideas with passengers, and one of his talks which always went well was "Europe from West to East" where he could share some interesting tales and humour from the Azores and Reunion, and many points in between.

He loved to tell the tale of a crafty captain during one stop at Reunion.

The ship had laid on shuttle buses to take passengers to and from the little town a short distance from the berthing point.

Apparently, the local taxi drivers had got wind of this and were miffed that a crop of lucrative fares would be taken from them.

The captain had advance information that the twenty local taxis would be parked across the dock gates to deny access to the fleet of shuttle buses.

When they docked, the captain told twenty of his crew to dress in civvies and take a taxi to the far side of island.

With the cabs out of the way, the shuttle operation worked fine.

When the taxis returned, the drivers came to the gangway as requested to sort payment from the captain.

In fluent French he told them to depart the scene and multiply, and pointed out that they had started the daft games and he was pleased to join in.

The posse of huge engine room guys standing behind him nodded their agreement.

He told the taxi drivers that, if they behaved themselves, he would happily mention their services on his next stop and give passengers the choice of a shuttle bus or a private taxi.

Honour was satisfied, kind of, but the captain also learned some French expressions which were new to him.

John liked most of the people he'd met; they'd worked hard and were going to enjoy travelling in style and spending their money before the government, or the kids, snaffled the lot.

John's skills weren't required on what he thought of as the kiddie cruises where people danced and drank all night and slept all day.

Then again, sometimes the kids could be well outdone by the older set.

One of John's best cruise memories came courtesy of a Saga ship. These ships were getting rid of their image as floating rest homes and their passengers from fifty upwards could show some of the youngsters how to party.

Every comedian knew the gags and nobody minded much when SAGA was defined as being an acronym for Sex Annually, Generally August. Or that even the portholes were bifocal and so on.

As it happened, one of the most memorable cruise trips ever came on a Saga trip to the Caribbean when the ship anchored just off Port Antonio in Jamaica.

The crew had set up a superb lunch on the beach and the wine and rum flowed in the hot sunshine. There was even a champagne raft berthed just a few steps into the warm water.

By the time the passengers took tenders back to the ship at around six, the atmosphere was infectious.

Quick showers were followed by after-sun lotion and dinner and John rose to his feet to speak to a mightily receptive audience to make a great atmosphere magical.

The house band caught the mood and changed location from the main lounge to the deck. By one in the morning, a lovely mix of passengers and crew were bouncing around to the greatest hits of the Sixties.

An American cruise ship passed at close quarters, and it was clear that the boring thirty somethings on deck were checking stock market prices on their phones.

Next day John heard, and he hoped it was true, that the captain of the boring ship had phoned his opposite number on Saga to complain about the noise.

Of course, the Caribbean rum and sunshine led to other results which weren't always so happy.

One memorable evening, in the early hours, John and Janet's nightcaps were interrupted by two chaps in their eighties fighting on the floor of the bar – over a woman, also in her eighties.

The way it had come about was something of a classic.

Chap number one had gone to the loo, and chap number two was trying to ask the lady what she thought of the cruise. He had a sore throat and a very quiet voice and was straining to make conversation, especially as the lady was more than a little deaf.

The sight which greeted chap one on his return was of a stranger with, apparently, his tongue in his wife's ear. Rather than make enquiries, he decked him, as you do.

A bit taken by surprise, the lady kicked the innocent man as he went down. It wasn't clear whether the couple did this as a routine in younger days, but, either way, they were taken down to the ship's brig while the other poor chap was taken away for medical treatment.

The next day, the two Horlicks louts were put off the ship to make their own way home, and the recipient of the attack proudly toured the ship showing off his black eye and telling the tale.

John suggested to the captain that he might like to arrange for head office to release the story to the media and raise the profile of mature cruising by several notches – he didn't.

Now and again, a funny scene popped up out of the blue which suggested that there was a lord of comedy up there pulling the strings, particularly when older passengers were on board.

Quite often, the evening would end with the ship's house band performing on the top deck under starry skies in tropical waters.

Sometimes, passengers were knackered after a busy day ashore or the sheer hard work involved in eating, drinking, and sunbathing.

This sometimes meant that the audience would have really thinned out by the time the band was into its last contracted hour leading up to midnight.

One late night, John was up on deck enjoying a particularly good band as he relaxed with a cognac warming in his hand.

They had played a string of middle of the road pop, but were now cutting loose as most of the audience had sloped off to their beds.

There were two distinct groups of audience members remaining.

At the front were about twenty or so fans who were enjoying the sounds, with some of them even dancing.

Towards the back, well away from the "noise" of the band were about twenty hardy souls who clearly weren't enjoying it much, but thought they may as well listen a bit longer as it was included in the fare they had paid.

Many of them had sticks and walking frames propped against their tables too.

The band, though, were clearly going down well with the livelier group at the front who were all in favour of the band letting rip and breaking into rockier and more vibrant numbers.

The top deck was well away from any cabins where passengers were sleeping and they could really jack up the volume.

The front end of the audience loved this – it was now sounding more like a rock concert than a tea dance.

The long-suffering bunch at the back were clearly not so keen.

The band broke into a brilliant driving beat lead by their splendid bass and drum players as they launched into Michael Jackson's *Thriller*.

Fans of the superb video which went with the late

Michael's best-selling hit will remember the chilling scene when zombies rise from their graves and stomp menacingly as they advance towards the camera.

This was clearly in the bands' heads too – and explained why they were doing well to play while weeping with laughter.

The people at the back had had enough of this loud stuff and were walking slowly forward in a group, and they had to head towards the band on their way to bed.

Sadly, no video camera was around, or a huge YouTube hit would have been generated by sight of a group of walking frame and stick wielding oldies plodding forward in perfect time with *Thriller*.

The range of cruise styles was huge and John's niche was the market for the "mature" traveller.

It was clear that the style and background of passengers varied a lot; often depending on the departure port and the cruise line, even on the individual ship.

Some guests were clearly affluent and some were keeping a tight budget and not spending much beyond there all-inclusive packages.

Some of the lines put on very short "taster cruises" of one or two nights and these worked well as marketing tools.

Those new to a cruise ship would be offered a discount on a longer cruise and many would take it up, having enjoyed their brief experience of life on board.

Some of these tasters turned into a mini booze cruise.

On one ship, John was leaving Newcastle, well North Shields technically, en route to fourteen nights around the Baltic.

On the first night out, about five hundred people would be doing the full itinerary, but another seven hundred would be on for one night only to Dundee.

They would then disembark at Dundee for a coach trip back to Tyneside, most of them fast asleep after a recently completed twelve hour drinking session.

The passengers staying on to the Baltic would be happy to see them leave the ship and be replaced by several hundred more sedate Scots also looking forward to some beautiful scenery.

By late night on that first evening out from Newcastle, the "taster" passengers had clearly tasted a fair amount of alcohol. Many of then looked as if they had kicked off with vodka on the porridge, followed by a long liquid lunch, and now a major top-up at the ship's busy bars.

That was one piece of the jigsaw in a combination which John recognised as another cunning plan from that comedy genius in the sky.

The duo on stage were two good looking girls from the Ukraine with decent voices and backing tracks. Their English was good, and a bit accented, and they were doing fine in belting out pop classics which suited the party animals perfectly.

Then they started a song which has a bit of history, especially in the north east of England.

Living Next Door to Alice was a big hit for a band called Smokie. It was a bouncy tale of a chap pining for a lost love and had a great sing-along chorus.

For reasons lost in the mists of time, a rather different version had been recorded by one of Middlesbrough's finest exports, the comedian Chubby

Brown.

In the unlikely event you don't know of "Chubs", suffice to say that he is one of the most successful blue comedians ever.

In his real life persona of Roy Vasey, he is one of the most gentle and considerate chaps you could ever meet.

When he dons his costume of bright patchwork suit and flying helmet (an obvious combination), he becomes a totally different animal.

Many of his gags are too strong for this book (bloody hell – editor).

He regularly sells out big venues in places like Blackpool, often with an audience where women are in the majority. The only complaints he receives are that they think he's sometimes not blue enough.

As he makes his entrance, so to speak, the audience would usually chant "You fat bastard."

The Royal Shakespeare Company it is not, but it's a winning formula.

In the original song, the chorus ends with "Living next door to Alice …….." followed by a very usable pause for the purposes of the Chubs version.

He would have his audience gleefully singing along "Alice, Alice, who the fuck is Alice?"

It became such a popular part of his act that it was recorded and sold really well.The Ukrainian duo on the cruise ship would know nothing of this.

It was something of a shock for them, then, when they reached the pause in the chorus of their plaintive love song and over six hundred Geordies stood up as one and delivered the essential missing line.

They looked at each other in open-mouthed surprise and missed the next verse completely as the backing track continued without them.

To their credit, they got back into it and finished the song.

Their next link was good;

"We are now going to sing a lovely song called *Lady in Red* and wonder which bad words you will shout during this one."

Like many of the passengers, the girls would have quite a story to tell when they arrived home.

CHAPTER 8 – COMIC CUTS

As somebody once said, comedy is a serious business, and John would see the sense in that and love to analyse the business with fellow professionals.

There was no better place than on a cruise ship and he looked forward to catching up with many of the regulars who trod the boards of ships' theatres.

As a regular now, he had got to know many of them well, and it was a fine pleasure to sit late at night and kick ideas around with people who really understand what it was all about.

They genuinely did share philosophical debate on comedy and the meaning of life, but there were some great tales of triumphs and disasters too – and memories of great characters.

One evening, John was sitting with comedians Barry and Les, two very funny guys, and you could sense the itching in their three heads to share the latest gossip. They were soon joined by Cruise Director Debbie, ready for a bit of relaxation after another non-stop day.

That job was sheer hard work and people who thought it might be a working holiday didn't stay long. To do it well meant being busy most of the day and late into the evening – everything from compering and performing on stage to running a programme of daytime activities and a host of shore excursions when the ship was in port.

Sometimes Debbie's heart sank when poor performers came on board, but, with these three guys at the top of their game, life was that bit easier.

Debbie had a fine sense of humour and clearly had

friends of a similar taste whose tales she passed on with great relish.

Modern communications and social media meant that she often entertained with news from pals on other ships and at home. Carefully keeping an eye so that no passengers could over-hear their chat, she revelled in launching into sheer filth, when necessary to the story, which it often was.

She also had the wordsmith's gift of enjoying alliteration – and used it well.

Flopping down with a cool glass of wine, she was straight into action.

"I've ruined my mascara after ten minutes on the phone with Mucky Margaret from Manchester" she said.

The three guys perked up. They'd never met the lady, but a string of Debbie stories about her meant that they knew that comedy gold was in the offing, especially in Margaret's instant reviews of chaps she'd had flings with – and there was a large cast of them by the sound of it.

"I saw her for a night out in Liverpool last time we docked there" began Debbie and she'd had a great chap the night before. Into her like a brylcreemed rat up a greasy drainpipe she said"

Probably not an assessment that would make either Trip Advisor or Mills and Boon.

"It went downhill after that though" continued Debbie.

"We went for a meal and then to a pub and this guy was chatting her up. I had to get away to re-join the ship, but I told Mucky Margaret that he was a waste of time – clearly ratted and no use to her."

"She's just told me on the phone that I was right. He

took her back to his hotel and couldn't do a thing. She said it was like trying to push a marshmallow into a money box."

The table dissolved into gales of laughter and, as Barry pointed out, the conversation sounded so like the home life of our dear Queen.

Like John, the company around the table had been in the business for a long time now, and they still marvelled at how comparatively tame things had become, sometimes for the better, and wept with laughter at what used to be considered acceptable a few decades back.

Quite rightly, a lot of racist and other offensive material had been given the chop, but it was frustrating when po-faced individuals of today tried to impose modern standards on an age which has gone.

"Do you know?" said Barry, "in about 1980 or so, I was at black tie dinner waiting to do a turn at the end of the night, and a government minister was making a speech."

"He did the usual political stuff and told them what fine people they were and then cracked a few gags which seemed to concentrate on birds with big tits and which nationalities had the biggest dicks. Nobody batted an eyelid and then he finished off with a gag which would have landed him in court now."

"He said he'd just been on a visit to Birmingham and was delighted to see that they'd cut all the trees down in the city centre so that "they" would have to walk to work like everybody else."

"It brought the house down – it would have been the lead story on the BBC today."

John chipped in with a TV programme he'd seen recently where some snotty woman had played a series of clips from programmes made in the Eighties which had running gags on the horrors of a black family living next door and the rest. The programme consisted of lining up some Z list celebs to pull faces and say how awful it all was.

"The trouble is, "said Les, "is that your snotty TV woman wasn't even born then and she wouldn't know that revolutions can happen in odd ways."

"Do you remember Charlie Williams? He was a cracking comic – and being a black guy on TV was unusual when he started. The clever thing was that he was from Barnsley and had a Yorkshire accent, so even the racists could accept him.

One of his favourite gags was to point at a white guy in the audience and tell him that his house was worth less than his own. The guy would ask for the reason, and Charlie would tell him that the Williams family didn't have a black guy living next door. It worked.

It was a bit like Till Death Do Us Part – the Alf Garnett character was such an over the top parody of a racist that it taught lessons without people noticing."

"Only snag is" said Barry, "some people nodded along with Alf and thought he was right."

"Best thing I've seen for a bit" said Les, "was Jim Davidson being interviewed by one of the snooty cow brigade and he handled in superbly."

They showed some clips of his TV shows from ages back and tut-tutted about him demeaning women and his characters like Chalky, the comedy West Indian guy.

The woman asked him if he wanted to apologise and

Jim said "Who to? The people who packed out the theatres, the people who gave me awards, or the people who pissed themselves laughing."

"Does it occur to you that, in fifty years from now, somebody might show a clip of you on TV and tell you that got it all wrong?"

"The snag is" said Les "is that the pendulum has swung too far to the politically correct side. Even a genius like Mel Brooks reckons that a brilliant film like Blazing Saddles couldn't be made today."

The discussion was becoming really philosophical now and Barry trumped them all when he'd announced that he'd seen a brilliant quotation by the author PD James in a newspaper recently.

"I actually tore it out and kept it." Praise indeed.

Reaching into an over-stuffed trouser pocket, he finally found his bit of research wedged between a crop of bar receipts.

Her we go;

"I believe that political correctness can be a form of linguistic fascism, and it sends shivers down the spine of my generation who went to war against fascism."

From the Paris Review, 1995, he concluded, sounding like a University professor, which he did resemble in his thoughtful moments.

All four of them round the table were great readers, partly because they were intelligent people who loved word, and partly because reading on cruise ships was the perfect switch-off from a busy life.

The debate ranged from the Thought Police in George Orwell's 1984 to the techniques of Hitler and Stalin in controlling the thinking of their subservient people.

They could have done with a counter-argument from someone who thought that political correctness was a good thing, but there was nobody at hand.

"The thing is" said John "proper comedians like you two can get the line right. You know you can't be anywhere near blue on a cruise ship, but you know how to make comedy happen inside the audience's heads. "

It was a simple fact of life that a comedian rarely got through a cruise without a complaint coming in. Every joke had the power to be offensive if you were looking for it and you had to grin and bear it.

Les had a good routine about mixing up heads in a mortuary – as you do. Sure enough, somebody took the trouble to call in to reception and log a complaint on the grounds that there had been a death in his family. On a cruise ship, he was unlikely to be the only one with recent funeral experience.

Oddly enough, Barry had a crop of good lines featuring Viagra and condoms and rarely an eyebrow was raised.

He loved the gag about the chap who was about to have a wisdom tooth removed and had the bad news from the dentist that he was completely out of any form of anaesthetic. He was offered two Viagra tablets instead – so that he'd have something to hang on to if the pain became too much.

This usually led straight to the one about the 99 year old granddad being prescribed Viagra.

At least it stopped him from pissing on his slippers.

The one that the audiences really seemed to love was Barry's tale of his neighbours who had taken to using luminous condoms – and leaving the curtains open at night.

Apparently, it's like watching a fridge door opening and closing, but quickly.

"They're good though" chipped in Les, "if you want to read in bed, and she doesn't."

Les continued with what he still thought was the best cruise ship gag ever although he could never tell it to an audience, unless the lottery money came in.

The other three had heard versions of this story before, but they loved hearing a master craftsman putting his spin on it.

Les took a breath and delivered the lines with the same concentration for an audience of three as he would for the London Palladium.

One quiet afternoon on board, most of the passengers are on shore doing trips and the ship's orchestra take the chance to use the empty theatre to run through a few new routines.

A passenger wanders in to listen and the whole band recognise him. He almost lives on the ship and has two things which mark him out – his shiny gold loyalty club badge and his little dog. Lord knows how they did the paperwork to get a dog on board, but, with the thousands he spent with the cruise line, anything seemed possible.

When the band leader calls a five-minute break, Mr Loyalty takes the chance to wander across.

"That's a lovely grand piano" he said, "and it sounds great. Do you mind if I have a play?"

"Of course, you're most welcome" came the reply, just in case he complained and the whole orchestra was in trouble.

He played well and the tune he performed was absolutely gripping and powerful.

The hard-bitten players who were about to wander off for a smoke or some fresh air on deck all stopped to listen.

They rarely applauded the guest artistes on board, but they stood and clapped this guy, before talking in huddled, almost reverential, whispers.

"That was amazing," said the astonished leader, "but these guys have been everywhere and heard everything, but not one of them knows that tune."

"I'm not surprised" said the new performer, "I wrote it but nobody will publish it."

"Unbelievable," came the reply, "What's it called?"

"*Every time I shag you, you scream like a bitch.*"

The leader was realising that the mystery was now solved, when the little dog calmly walked across the stage, raised his leg and pissed down his light grey trousers.

"Hey" he shouted, "do you know your dog's just pissed on my leg?"

"Know it" he said, "I wrote it"

"Still love it" said Debbie and chipped in with a new one.

"One ship I worked on, we had a Hungarian band leader on board and he was convinced that the whole band was having a go at him behind his back and thought that he knew nowt. And he was right."

His English was not bad, but not perfect, and it went wrong when he called them all together for a clear the air session.

He waited for silence, rapped his baton on the lectern, and announced;

"Some of you think that I know fuck nothing – but I know fuck all!"

This was how the evening went – it was like a bidding war for the best story, or the added line to make a great tale better.

It was John's turn to up the stakes with his memorable night on a cruise to the Caribbean the winter before.

It had been a long trip – about a month from the UK to the lovely sunshine and back.

On the way home, a crop of sea days beckoned with only stops at the Azores and Lisbon to break the routine.

Cruise director Ricky had the safe idea of putting on a passengers' talent show on the way home and this was a regular success. Many on board clearly expected it and had brought costumes, sheet music and the rest with them. Their experience of musicals and amdram back home would serve them well.

The day before the big night, Ricky caught John on deck and asked for a favour.

"Look," he said, " I have ten acts lined up for the talent show and nine of them are songs from the musicals, apart from one passenger from Middlesbrough who wants to do some stand -up comedy.

He seems ok, but he's never been on a stage before. Could you give him a run through tomorrow morning when the theatre is dark and guide him through it?"

John was pleased to help and twenty minutes were spent the next morning in showing him how to use a microphone to best effect and how to get used to having a thousand faces staring at you in the ship's huge double-deck height theatre.

"Don't tell me your act" said John, "but slow it down, get hold of them early and, above all, don't do anything even remotely light blue – they won't like it."

For the show itself, John parked himself in the wings and watched the succession of musical theatre numbers before Middlesbrough man was introduced as the sixth act of the evening.

John gave him a thumbs-up and hoped for the best.

It wasn't forthcoming. He never took the audience with him and was visibly floundering as his nervousness made his average gags even worse.

Knowing that his time was nearly up, he went for it – he really did.

He launched into the gag about the three husbands from France, Italy, and Middlesbrough bragging about their romantic prowess.

"Oh bollocks" thought John, "it can't be the one I'm thinking of." Sadly, it was.

The story line was of the Frenchman describing how his love-making with his wife had led to her orgasming noisily as she floated a foot above the bed.

The Italian went one better and described his wife screaming with pleasure "a metre above ze bed."

John watched the old gag tottering to its horrific conclusion.

"That's nowt" said the aspiring but failing comic "the bloke from Middlesbrough had fifteen pints at the club and went home and shagged his wife. He took his tadger out and wiped it on the velvet curtains. She hit the roof."

From his seat in the wings, John had the perfect view of one thousand mouths hanging open in shocked silence.

Cruise Director Ricky bounded up onto the stage and frog-marched Middlesbrough man away from it all, to be followed by Sally from Surrey singing I Feel Pretty.

The next day, John saw the amateur comic, who didn't win by the way, in a lounge nursing a beer.

"How do you think it went?" he asked.

Recalling a line he'd heard many years before, he couldn't resist.

"You were shite son."

CHAPTER 9 - HANGING THE MONKEY AND
BONKING THE BARMAID

The day soon came when John, and still slightly disbelieving Janet, were due to fly off to Las Vegas in real style.

John's admiring contact at the Civil Engineers' dinner had been as good as his word and had fixed business class flights, a top hotel, and a penthouse holiday as well as the splendid fee.

A couple of days before the trip, John was due a catch-up in a favourite Hartlepool pub and, despite the years of trains and boats and planes under his belt, he still enjoyed the company of old friends with a shared history.

They met on the Headland in the Fisherman's, known to all locally as simply "The Fish", and, on a late winter evening, this had a distinctive cosiness.

John's friends Terry and Alan were in the company and, as witnesses to the historic occasion of John's launch into the top end of the speaking circuit, they felt a pride in his success.

The pub was close to the sea and its wall decorations were perfect – artefacts and pictures of local fishing boats and lifeboats which were the real thing – not some artificial bits supplied by a pub chain designer.

John had always loved the now fashionable Danish idea of "hygge" – the feeling you get from sitting round a fire with good friends while hearing the icy rain rattling the windows.

John loved this place, famous for a warm welcome and often with top quality live music. John was no mean guitarist himself and would often chip in on the "open mic" nights when he could perch on a bar stool and deliver selections from his, largely Sixties, repertoire.

John remembered younger days when a pub like this would be a refuge for Scandinavian fishermen who had come into port to escape a North Sea storm.

Wonderfully, the locals and their temporary guests would be speaking in a language which wasn't English, Danish, Swedish or Norwegian. It probably couldn't be written down, but its lovely sound was a slice of living history.

If you had a north-east accent learning Danish or its sister languages wasn't difficult.

A Geordie would say "I'm gannen yem to the bairns" – I'm going home to the children – and it sounded almost identical in Danish.

The many visitors from such countries coming to Newcastle for cheap shopping were amazed that the locals seemed to speak Danish so well.

Living in the north east meant that Scandinavia felt like the preferred neighbour compared to the southern love affair with France.

Hartlepool had its own track record with that race.

Hanging, literally, above the bar was a monkey, and visitors from the south often wondered what kind of weird sadism was behind such an odd sight.

Those born in Hartlepool were known as monkey-hangers and wore the name as a badge of pride, or sometimes as the excuse for a Saturday night fight.

Even most people from odd southern parts, like York, knew the story which had its roots in Napoleonic times.

There was a threat of a French invasion on the East Coast and locals were told to keep a sharp watch.

Most people had never seen a Frenchie, and in the absence of mass media – and reading – had to rely on folk tales which summarised them as strange and ugly.

In those days, many ships carried a monkey as a mascot, kitted out in uniform or national dress.

And so it was that an unfortunate monkey fell overboard from a French ship east of Hartlepool and was washed ashore.

He was found gasping on the beach, a stone's throw from where The Fish now stood, and his lack of English and, crucially, his sporting of a stripy jumper marked him out as a spy for Napoleon.

To be fair, he was given a comprehensive trial by the local magistrates and, having nothing to say in his defence, was sentenced to hang.

The tradition for weird humour lived on and Terry leant in towards John and said, "Don't look now but do you see that bloke behind me in the red striped shirt looking half pissed?"

You might not recognise him now, but that's Teddy Garbutt – do you remember his stag night?"

It all came back now, even though Teddy looked ancient and bloated, not like the sharp young man about town who had entered local legend just up the hill from here.

They had been friends since school days, and, to major surprise, along came the news of wedding bells. She wasn't even pregnant – which constituted posh in these parts.

Before the fashion for stag nights in distant European

cities, Teddy had announced that he wanted a pub crawl around his beloved pubs on the Headland.

He wasn't really a drinker, though he thought he was, and a long stream of well-wishers' drinks in nearly a dozen pubs had left him with a bleary smile on his confused little face – a bit like tonight.

The other odd thing about Teddy was that he was useless at conversation but hated a silence.

His unusual technique was to lean forward to a member of the company and announce something, indeed anything, that they had in common.

He might tap you on the shoulder and announce that he too was wearing black shoes – not quite up to Oscar Wilde standards of conversational brilliance, but he was happy enough.

On the famous stag night, the universe had arranged a clever alignment.

By the time the stag party of about a dozen had reached the Shipbuilders' Arms, Teddy was leaning on the bar for support when he managed to recognise the landlord, Jeff Johnson, who had his arm around a pretty blonde lady who was his barmaid, and now his fiancée.

Sadly, Teddy also recognised the lady behind the bar as a previous conquest and what he said next was not designed to cause trouble, but merely to fill a conversational gap.

Smiling at landlord Jeff, he nodded to his fiancée and asked, "Isn't that Julie Armstrong?"

"Indeed, it is" he agreed.

"Oh" said Teddy, "I've shagged her as well!"

With tactical speed which would have impressed an

international rugby coach, six of the party yanked Teddy out into the street, while the rest blocked the bar hatch to prevent Jeff from organising another Hartlepool execution.

"He didn't mean any harm Jeff" was not a perfect explanation, but it was the best they could manage.

"Hell, I remember that night like it was yesterday," said John, "we've certainly shared some cracking times together."

"It's probably why there have been so many great comics from our patch" said Terry, "you just had to keep your eyes and ears open for what was happening around you – people like Bobby Thompson could do that."

Few names in the north east could produce warm nostalgia like the mention of this guy – known to all as "the little waster."

A tiny bloke, he would come on stage wearing the traditional "gansey" the close-knit and weatherproof top worn by local fishermen for centuries.

His comedy was very much rooted in his local community and it didn't work in the south of England for sure. They tried him on national television, but his strong accent and dialect words meant that people genuinely wanted sub-titles.

He wasn't just funny; he had an observational comedy style long before the trendy comedians filled arenas with it.

He told a lovely story about the unfairness of being a child in hard times.

His mam told him that the next day there would be seven people around the table for Sunday dinner (served at lunch-time of course) but she only had six pork chops.

"When I ask who would like a pork chop, you have to say, "no thank you mother" and then there'll be enough to go round."

Sunday dinner came and it worked well for the company and the catering when young Bobby declined his chop as instructed.

Main course plates were cleared away and mam asked "Who would like some trifle?"

"Yes, please mam" smiled a slightly hungry Bobby.

"You're not getting any – you wouldn't eat your pork chop."

The happy audiences loved it – even if they'd heard Bobby's routine many times before. In fact, Bobby himself said that people complained if he tried new material.

They loved the surreal tale of Hitler queueing up in the local chip shop – "there'll be war on" and, of course the vintage tale of the carrier bag.

In those days, bags were made of tough brown paper with string handles and lasted a lot longer than the plastic bags which were to come later. Unless it rained of course, when they didn't.

Everyone knew the answer when Bobby's wife asked him to mend the string on her bag.

"Well, I'm no engineer."

Perhaps the line which summed up his act best was when he gazed at the audience and, holding his hand on his forehead, announced "I'm in debt up to here – I wish I was tarler."

Debt rang a bell with many members of the audience, especially his financial analysis which proclaimed that "posh people have credit, but we have debt."

The lovely thing is that, long after Bobby's death, his CDs and DVDs still sell in huge numbers at the lovely Windows Music Store in the centre of Newcastle – many of them flying around the world as welcome Christmas presents which bring a taste of home to far-flung Geordies.

"Do you know?" said John, "I was reminiscing about Bobby when I bumped into Tim Healy at a do in Newcastle only a few weeks back."

Tim had gone on to great television success, especially in the Geordies to Germany bricklayer saga, Auf Wiedersehen Pet.

Long before that, though, he had started his career in the workies' clubs which John and his friends remembered fondly.

Tim had told John the story of his negotiation skills in the days when his reputation really took off.

In the early days when a comic would be happy to get £20 for a gig, Tim was going great guns and getting up to £75, with the clubs knowing that they'd make a lot more than that at the bar when he was on.

A concert secretary had phoned one day and checked a date to see if Tim was free. He was.

"Champion" said Mr Secretary, "will £20 do yer?"

"Sorry" said Tim, "I'm getting £75 these days."

"Bollocks to that" came the reply," we're not paying that much for a bloody comedian!"

"Well, if you don't mind" said Tim, "I'll leave this one – I'm sure another booking will come in for that date."

"I'll go to £30" said Mr Secretary who had set his

heart on Tim performing at his club.

"Sorry" said Tim, "it's £75."

"Tell you what, son," came back the offer which closed the deal, "£45 and you win the raffle."

"Done."

CHAPTER 10 – BEAVER LAS VEGAS

John had allocated the day after his Headland pub reunion for a bit of wake-up time and to supervise Janet packing for the dream trip to Vegas.

Their generous American host had organised flights on Virgin Upper Class direct from London Gatwick and they were drooling at the prospect.

"Bloody hell," said John, "these videos of the Virgin Clubhouse look amazing."

As experienced travellers by now, they had learned to expect the unexpected and liked to travel down the day before and leave a couple of days at the end of the trip so that there was no panic if a delay cropped up.

John had dabbled with Yoga, and Janet was a big fan of Tai Chi, and there was something in the old philosophies about staying calm, changing what you could, and accepting what you couldn't.

Whether it was in the air, on the railway, or at sea, grumbling and moaning wasn't going to change much. John always carried the book he was reading with him or did some notes for comedy ideas, so time was never really lost.

He was a very regular traveller on the East Coast mainline trains from the North East to London and accepted that things would go wrong.

Most of the travel investment still went south and the cramped lines from the north meant that one broken down train could scupper the whole lot.

Sometimes, there was tragedy involved and someone ending his life in front of a high-speed train always produced a chill.

One time that happened, and there were a few, a self-important passenger moaned out loud that his day was now ruined because of the anticipated delay into King's Cross Station.

The passing train guard wisely observed, "The poor bloke dead on the line has probably had better ones, sir."

The delay before "sir" said it all.

The guard was on his way to comfort the train driver, knowing that many people who had seen a suicide at close quarters could never face taking charge of a train again.

Sometimes late arrivals were for mechanical rather than human reasons, and all you could do was, literally, grin and bear it.

If John was going to London for one of his regular lunch speaking gigs, he preferred to go down the night before, rather than have an early morning start and arrive feeling knackered. It also meant that late arrivals could be laughed at rather than fretted over.

On one occasion, he'd left Darlington at 4.30, planning to be in London by about 7 to enjoy some television and a glass of wine before a good night's sleep.

Around York, the train was making odd noises and then stopped. The announcement came over that all was now well.

It wasn't.

The train conked out again near Doncaster and they had to send for the wonderfully named breakdown locomotive – the Thunderbird.

That made it to just north of Peterborough before that failed too.

The passengers all had to wait on the platform for the next south bound train and John eventually reached his bed at the Hilton at almost eleven 'o'clock.

There had been times when airlines went wrong too and John's buffered timetable planning meant he could almost enjoy such occasions.

On one trip, he had been speaking at a travel trade dinner in lovely Copenhagen and was due to catch the quick lunch-time flight the next day from Kastrup Airport to Newcastle.

The small plane took off and levelled out. Just as coffee was about to be served, the most horrendous noise came from the passenger door at the front of the cabin.

Very calmly the Danish pilot announced, in perfect English then Danish, "Do not be alarmed, we are safe. A seal has parted around the door and we are going back to the airport as a precaution. We shall be on the ground in just a few minutes."

Across the narrow aisle from John, an old Danish lady was clearly terrified and hyper-ventilating.

John's basic Danish kicked in and, reaching over the narrow aisle, he cuddled the lady and told her "Alt er fint" – everything's fine.

The co-pilot walking down the aisle chipped in, "Glad to hear it sir."

The plane went back to Kastrup quite safely, and the passengers were offered dinner and an overnight in the lovely Hilton right on the airport.

When John and Janet were logged in, they came up as regular stayers Diamond Members and were given the penthouse overlooking the beautiful Oresund Bridge between Denmark and Sweden.

They spent a lovely couple of hours enjoying a bottle of wine and watching the traffic on this five-mile long engineering marvel which joined Malmo in Sweden with the Danish capital Copenhagen.

It was a combined road and rail bridge, and even incorporated a long tunnel which passed under the airport runways.

Travel hitches like this were to be welcomed, and the next day they were back home.

If you just accepted that every trip by air was going to be an experience, you could relax and let it happen – like the time John was arrested by the FBI, in Manchester.

That's Manchester, England.

When joining a cruise ship, he'd become used to the fact that the agent would send you joining instructions and you did as you were told.

For this trip, he was due to fly from Manchester to New York, stay overnight, then fly the next morning to Puerto Rico to join the ship.

Checking in was going fine until he was asked to report to the "enquiries desk."

He was greeted by a man mountain of a guy who looked like a former American Footballer player, which, it turned out, he was. He was in fact, one of the FBI's men on the ground at airports throughout the world.

In the current climate their job, understandably, was to detect any security alarm bells before they approached anywhere near the USA.

The routine with cruises was that the speaker was sent his outbound flight air tickets and would receive his homebound details just before leaving the ship.

As a result, the FBI computer picked up a crop of worrying aspects on John's profile.

It looked as if he was going to fly to the States and had no plans to come back - and his most recent passport entries included Cuba and the Middle East.

By now, John was sporting a greying beard and, as someone who tanned easily, he did look quite exotic – or shifty, whichever.

In the interview room, although he knew he was innocent, his voice went up several octaves and turned into Orville the Duck.

Happily, he had his cruise line contract at hand and was able to convince Mr Mountain that all was well.

"They pay you to go on cruises; no shit!"

Beautifully put.

As a result, John was now on the FBI approved travellers' list which felt like a result.

It didn't help much at Chicago's O'Hare Airport a few months later, but that was the fault of John's pet beaver.

To explain.

Like many north easterners, and worldwide too, John was a huge fan of Viz magazine. Though it's not as funny as it used to be (in joke), it was still miles ahead of most other attempts at cartoon comedy.

Regulars like the Fat Slags, Finbarr Saunders and Roger Mellie, the man on the telly, had John in gales of laughter. The one which really creased him, though, was Walter Weaver and His Band of Beavers.

This featured a young man on a tricycle who toured the country carrying a full marching band of beavers in his rear saddlebag.

They, like the best superheroes, would rescue the down-trodden and famously defeated an evil property developer who planned to demolish a school for colour blind children who would never play snooker or become electricians.

The beavers had built a mighty dam of twigs, all of a foot high, and that was the end of that.

The story ended with the beaver marching band playing a salute to the reprieved kids, with their traditional chorus of "eek, eek, eek."

As a member of the regional movers and shakers now, John often received invitations to some very pleasant evenings, and he was chuffed to bits to find himself at Viz's birthday party.

He was sharing some laughter with Chris Donald, one of the magazine's founders, when a new face joined the group.

"John" said Chris, "this is my good friend Simon Thorp."

"Wow," said John, "maximum respect. You are the guy who wrote Walter Weaver and His Band of Beavers."

He was convinced when John could quote the story line just about word for word.

They exchanged business cards and John was chuffed to bits when a cardboard tube arrived in the post a few days later.

It contained the *original* of the Beaver story – priceless to a fan.

Janet was a star at making soft toys and, for John's birthday, she produced Beaver, complete with tartan waistcoat and the special hat he wore for leading the marching band.

Young Beaver travelled the world with John and his waistcoat was soon studded with souvenir pins from his travels.

His proudest possession was his badge which appointed him as a representative of Canada, after a splendid evening at Canada House in Trafalgar Square. It's amazing what happens after fine hospitality and beautiful iced wine.

The day John and Beaver were changing planes in Chicago would live long in the memory.

John was queuing to check in, with Beaver peeping out of his cabin bag taking in the atmosphere.

Like many American airports, beagle dogs were on the prowl, sniffing out drugs and other forbidden substances in hand luggage.

One of them jumped on to John's bag, at the floor by his feet, and manage to trigger the loud squeak which Janet had thoughtfully fitted.

The dog started barking at some volume and with John, and Beaver, trying to look innocent, were surrounded by a posse of armed police.

"No problem," pleaded John, "your dog was interfering with my beaver."

That was no help, but order was soon restored.

Perhaps John's most surreal airline experience came some way from the land of the free when he was scheduled to join a cruise ship in Cuba.

As usual, the cruise line had supplied economy class tickets from London to Havana, and, as it was a long flight, John wondered about sorting an upgrade.

He phoned the airline and explained his request, and

the answer was like something from the pen of George Orwell.

"No comrade," came the response, "we are a socialist country and we believe that class divisions are typical of the capitalist running dogs who are the opposite of our culture."

"I understand completely" said John diplomatically, "but I've looked at the cabin plans for your planes and there seem to be a dozen seats at the front which look very like first class spacing."

"They are not first class sir, they are seats supplied as a mark of gratitude to supporters of the revolution."

Catching on quickly, John asked, "How can my wife and myself become supporters of the revolution?"

"It's a thousand dollars each comrade."

Sorted.

After some experience of travelling at the posh end of planes, John concluded that it was a bit like listening to music on top end equipment instead of a dated radio.

Once you'd experienced the best, it was hard to go back.

There was no flight from Newcastle to Gatwick, so they flew to Heathrow where the Virgin chauffeur picked them up and whisked them to the Clubhouse, which lived up to expectations and then some.

Check in floated by, and a couple of hours of cocktails, fine food and a spa treatment definitely beat the usual hubbub of an airport.

Halfway through the eleven hour flight, John turned to Janet and said, "How good is this?"

After a restaurant quality meal over the Atlantic,

they enjoyed more wine and a cognac, before the seat was flipped over into a very comfortable bed.

Their American host had fixed a flight which would have them landing at Las Vegas's McCarran Airport at night and he had that spot on.

The incredible last leg over completely bare and dark desert ended with the amazing sight of the lights of the Vegas Strip with towers of light shining high into the sky.

For the working part of the trip, they were allocated a beautiful room in the Hilton on the Strip where the conference was being held and John's speaking appearances went like a dream.

He wondered a little if his humour would translate to the American corporate market, but his homework and experience meant that he was a monster success and he knew that lots more work would follow.

After a few days of "work", their host provided a stretch limousine to take them to the promised penthouse for their add-on holiday.

Their welcome included a lovely letter of praise from their host and a "I'll fix lunch before you guys have to go and we'll sort out your future engagements here; I have an agent buddy who'd like to meet you if that's ok."

Hell, yes, it certainly was.

Despite the gambling reputation of the place there was so much more to do and they lived the dream around the shops, the restaurants and the incredible hotels and theatres.

A card under their door one day invited them to attend a presentation on "time share opportunities". They didn't think they wanted one, but John said, "Let's go along – I love watching American sales techniques – I'm sure I can learn a lot."

He was right too – beautifully done, special temptations and the rest, and they were given a $100 voucher to use in the casino just for attending.

They managed to resist the best attempts of the super sales team to get them to sign on the dotted line, but John loved to learn and he'd gained a great free tutorial.

They came back from a day out in the first week, and found an envelope with a message from their host – if you guys are free on Friday, I've fixed you a trip to the Grand Canyon.

That was another special day, and clearly done in the best style.

A stretch limo, what else, picked them up for the drive to Boulder City Airport where they boarded a helicopter which flew them over the Hoover Dam on the way to the Canyon.

Beaver, being an expert on dams, was along for the ride too and professed himself suitably impressed with the magnificent dam which was a lifeline for water and power for the enormous demands of Vegas.

The view of the magnificent Grand Canyon lived up to the hype and was made even better when the helicopter dropped the long way to the canyon's floor and they stepped out for champagne and canapes.

At the end of an unforgettable day, they arrived back at their hotel late in the evening and, feeling tired and dusty, were ready for a shower and crashing out for an early night.

Like most hotels in Vegas, you didn't simply walk into the foyer and into the lift to your room. They were cleverly designed so that you had to navigate through slot machines and other gambling temptations.

John was feeling for the room key in his shirt pocket when he came across the casino voucher which he'd almost forgotten.

"Look at this" he said, "it expires at midnight – let's use it so we can say we gambled in Vegas."

The only game which John half understood was roulette, and he'd read an article about it on the plane journey.

Janet was keener on crashing out, but John persuaded her, "I'll put the $100 on a single number – it's 36 to 1 and won't win, but so what?"

Feeling like a dusty James Bond, he leaned across the proper gamblers and put his stake on 28, his birthday.

Perhaps the best way to gamble is to try to lose quickly, because the ball jumped and popped and landed in the 28 slot.

They collected their $3700 dollars and cashed it in before heading upstairs.

They threw off their shoes in their luxurious accommodation and looked at each other.

"I wonder if this is all a dream" John thought out loud.

"I wonder if we'll be marked out as Mr and Mrs Big," said Janet, "one bet and a big win before cashing in. They are probably checking the cc tv right now."

From what John knew of gambling levels in Vegas, and Casino was one of his favourite films, they were nowhere near the top end of the scale.

The next morning, enjoying a leisurely breakfast on

their air-conditioned balcony, John was reading the Las Vegas Review and saw that Terry Clayton was on stage at Hooters that evening.

This man had won the American stand-up comedy award twice.

After the time share presentation, John was looking forward to continuing his American education.

The Hooters Bar, with casino and hotel attached of course, was something else. They'd heard of these places but seeing it for real was still hard to believe.

The place was absolutely packed with beer drinking party people, as many women as men, and featuring waitresses with tight white t shirts and even tighter orange shorts.

The slogan on the backs of the shirts made John laugh out loud, "Delightfully tacky, yet unrefined."

In some ways, it reminded John of those north eastern working men's clubs all those years ago, but there was something almost antiseptic about the place too. Many Americans had an almost prudish side to them and this place felt safe rather than risky.

The poor young comedian who warmed up for the big star did not do well. Waving his stick microphone like a magic wand, perhaps hoping to make the evening disappear, he wandered up to a redneck guy sitting near the front.

"Where are you from sir?"

"Chicago," he grunted.

"And what do you do for a living?"

"I'm an engineer. What do you do?"

Nearly one thousand people groaned in sympathy,

and the trainee entertainer wisely decided to say his thanks and slink backstage to lick his wounds.

Terry Clayton bounded on and did really well.

What surprised John was that his act was not unlike a Les Dawson routine from years back – mother-in-law gags and music hall classics along the lines of "I wouldn't say that my wife was heavy but when I carried her over the threshold, I had to make three trips."

The audience loved him, and John had learned something new – even if the gags weren't.

The farewell lunch went well and, along with the new American agent on board, life looked very good indeed.

The return journey via stretch limo and luxury air travel felt like the new normal.

CHAPTER 11 – THIS SPORTING LIFE

Big name sports figures and the speaking circuit had always been an obvious match, and John was initially surprised to discover that many of them liked to, figuratively anyway, have a hand to hold in front of a big audience.

It seemed odd at first when you remembered that many of these guys had performed at huge sports grounds with enormous attendances, but an after-dinner audience was clearly a different challenge.

John had built quite a following for events like this and had a reliable format. He would conduct a Parkinson style interview on stage in the first half of the evening and draw out some lovely memories and funny tales.

After the comfort break, he would field questions from the floor and usually auction a few personally signed shirts courtesy of the celebrity and have the evening well in the black for the organiser.

One evening in Bristol, the audience questions turned into comedy gold.

A big-name rugby player, Freddie Gray, was on stage with John and doing well.

One subject to avoid was the scurrilous gossip which claimed that Freddie was having a passionate fling with Shirley Griffiths, the teatime television presenter in the region.

As they were both married to other people, the subject would be a smidge delicate.

As it was a big audience of over 600, the plan was to distribute postcards at the interval and ask guests to write their name and question.

Ten minutes before the second half was due to begin, John was handed the huge pile of cards. He scanned them, gulped, and had a tactical planning chat with Freddie the rugby man.

Nearly every question was about the alleged affair and one card had a postscript, "By the way, I'm the main sponsor tonight and if you don't ask this question, I'm not paying up."

John started the second half with some funny warm-up material, all the time glancing at the huge fistful of cards in his left hand.

Every time he looked at them, the audience giggled like schoolkids and they were a fine comedy prop he wasn't expecting.

Eventually, with tension rising, and the audience as quiet as mice, he turned to Freddie and, with a deadpan expression, addressed him directly.

"I've never seen this before, Freddie. Over five hundred questions for you tonight, and many of them very similar."

"Too bloody true" you could hear the audience thinking as they smirked in anticipation.

"So" said John, "I'll try to combine them into one."

"Are you trying to get yourself into television in this region?"

The audience roared with laughter, and John's gaze swivelled to Mr Sponsor who nodded his approval.

Freddie paused like a pro and answered, "Well, yes, some of it."

With his ever-expanding experience of sporting partnerships, John learned that some stars were naturally gifted with people – and some were public relations disasters.

One of the best was Kevin Keegan, who, as manager of Newcastle United, really understood how important the club was to the daily life of Tyneside and beyond.

Not everyone concerned with football knew this, and some showed a positive flair for alienating their key supporters.

John remembered well an occasion in the Nineties when Kevin gave a perfect lesson in how to get it right.

John was due to compere a business launch literally on the banks of the Tyne with KK, as he was known, as guest of honour.

The event was to celebrate the fact that Northumbrian Water had completed the task of diverting all sewage to underground pipes, thus ending the previous practice of pumping the human waste and the rest directly into the Tyne which flowed through the centre of Newcastle.

Famously, some years back, a meeting of the City Council had to be ended because of the "horrific stink on a warm day."

Now, with a mammoth amount of money and civil engineering, the Tyne was sparking clean and fish were returning,

John called at St James's Park, the home of Newcastle United, to pick up Kevin and have a chat on the way to the riverside Copthorne Hotel where the event was being held.

The Copthorne was one of the first hotel chains to start to transform the derelict riverside, which had seen some years of neglect with the end of shipbuilding and heavy engineering

By the start of the twenty first century, the whole area looked superb, with the effectively twin cities of Newcastle and Gateshead boasting a host of hotels, restaurants, and fine entertainment venues like the Sage and the Baltic.

John loved to catch classic films like Get Carter and superb television like the Likely Lads to see how the river used to be, with myriads of cranes and big ships on the quayside.

The event at the Copthorne was not for the public, but for invited guests, but word soon spreads in Newcastle and a posse of fans were outside the hotel as John and Kevin left the car and walked towards reception.

One pair stood out – a proud dad and his son of about seven or so, both in the black and white striped replica shirts of the team they loved.

Kevin beamed at them and, star struck, neither dad nor lad could speak.

Some big names would have kept walking and ignored them, but not Super Kev.

"Brilliant to see you two," he said, "and thanks for your support – it's really important."

Focussing totally on the spellbound youngster, he asked "Why don't you come and see the lads train one day and meet everybody. Would you like that?"

He sure as hell would.

Kevin took a business card out of his pocket and gave it to the proud dad.

"There you go," he said, "your dad has my special

number now, so give me a ring when you'd like to come and meet everybody. But, and this is very important, it must be on a day when you are on holiday. School is too important to miss and you need to work hard. Do you promise to do that for me?"

"Yes, Mr Keegan, I promise" spluttered the young disciple.

The youngster and his dad walked off, feeling a foot above the ground. The whole exchange had taken a couple of minutes, but it was beautifully done.

Someone like Kevin was a natural, but John loved to see a sportsman blossom into a speaking talent from a standing start.

On one memorable occasion, that had come about by chance.

John was due to compere a charity fund-raiser in Newcastle with the big name football speaker, Tommy Docherty, due to come from across the Pennines and his Manchester home.

The day started out fine but then it snowed all afternoon. Despite his best efforts, the journey was impossible and it looked as if the evening might have a hole in the middle.

John was looking at options with the crestfallen organiser after a few phone calls had not borne fruit.

"Let's see your guest list" said John.

A scan through over six hundred names yielded a possible solution when John spotted the name of Peter Beardsley on the guest list.

John had had the pleasure of Peter's company at a few events and knew that his top-level football career and sharp understanding of the game would be a gold mine.

They decide not to ask him too early and waited until guests were seated and on their starters.

He went over to the table where Peter was sitting, nodded "hello" and told him the situation.

"It's a biggie for the charity and without a big football name it will feel flat – and they won't raise so much."

"I'd love to John," he said, "but I can't do that like you can."

"I'll tell you what. I'll get a couple of bar stools and a couple of microphones and I'll lead you through some of the great tales you've told me before. If it goes pear shaped, I'm supposed to be the pro, so it'll be my fault."

"Go on then," said Peter, "but I'll be crap."

As it turned out, he was brilliant.

John had heard him chatting privately before about memories of the great Sir Bobby Robson and knew that a north-east audience would love them.

It felt a bit like a game of tennis where John could lob up the ball and watch Peter smash it home.

It helped that John had a proper valuation of a top footballer's skill and intelligence. Some people could be arrogant about these top players and were themselves too thick to realise that intelligence came in different forms.

You wouldn't have a pop at Einstein because he never played professional football, would you?

At Peter's level, you could have a ball hit towards you at high speed and, with a defender at your back who could flatten you, you had a fraction of a second to weigh up an infinite number of options – then pick the right one and execute it.

That was intelligence too.

John talked this through and could tell that Peter appreciated it – and their mutual respect evolved into a brilliant double act in front of the audience's eyes.

Sir Bobby Robson, as a former manager of Newcastle United, was held in massive affection, and Peter wowed them with some tales of his former boss's earlier career.

One of Bobby's first forays into management had been with Ipswich Town, a small club at the time.

At his interview, Bobby told the Chairman that it would take time to build success at the club from a modest base.

"If you want instant success Mr Chairman, it's not going to happen. I'll need to start with your youngsters and go from there. If you haven't got time for that, let's shake hands and forget about my coming here."

The Chairman promised Bobby time and he was as good as his word.

The two of them worked together perfectly, despite their very different backgrounds. Bobby was proud of his relatively ordinary roots in the north east, while the Chairman had gone through a privileged upbringing – and sounded like it.

Peter brought the house down with his telling of what Bobby had told him about the evening when Ipswich celebrated the first signs of success, with their youth team bringing a trophy to the club.

They had organised a celebration dinner with the young champions in their smart club blazers looking as proud as the invited parents who sat by them.

As Bobby had told Peter, the Chairman, with his cut-glass accent, said something to the dinner which would have had a Geordie fired.

"This is a wonderful evening," he said, "and I'm as delighted as can be with this magnificent trophy in front of me, and these young men who have made us so proud of them."

Peter's telling of the story was made even funnier with his imitation of a posh accent instead of his usual Tyneside twang.

"But let's not make this a one-orf," said the Chairman.

"Years from now, I want to be celebrating another national youth trophy. When you mums and dads have had a jolly good evening of wining and dining as guests of the club, I want you to start producing our next generation of winners by going home and having a jolly good fack!"

This brought a huge round of applause, and Bobby always believed that if he'd tried that approach, he'd have been thrown out.

The audience and John beamed as it got better and better.

Before Sir Bobby passed away after an incredibly brave fight against multiple bouts of cancer, he proved his sheer class one more time.

John had helped on the testimonial committee for Micky Barron, a long serving player at Hartlepool United.

He had served as captain and long serving player and had been a terrific leader for the club on and off the pitch.

The usual format was for a succession of events including golf days and the like, with the centrepiece being a large dinner with a top football guest.

"Who would be your ideal guest?" John asked Micky.

"Bobby Robson would be amazing, but perhaps I'm aiming too high?"

As they say in the north-east, shy kids get nowt, so John phoned and tried.

"Be delighted" came Bobby's reply, "he's a great lad and I'd be glad to help."

A Thursday night was fixed in a good local venue, and Bobby's name on the flyer ensured a sell-out.

Not long before the big day, there came the sad news of the passing of fine Fulham and England footballer Johnny Haynes. Soon afterwards the funeral was announced as being in Edinburgh – the day after Micky's dinner date.

John phoned Bobby and, after expressing his sympathies, said, "We know you'll want to be at the funeral of course and we'll understand completely if you'll have to pull out of Micky's testimonial dinner."

"No chance son; I've promised to support the dinner and I will. I'll just need to set off early the next day, won't I?"

He was simply superb on the night – delivering a great two-way with John and praising Micky to the skies. He stayed right to the end and, rather than get away early as he had every right to do, he was shaking hands and posing for pictures well after midnight.

John discovered later that, after arriving home near Durham City, he had a couple of hours' sleep before catching the first train north to pay his respects to his old friend.

Like many truly great people, Bobby had real class. He had the magic touch of treating all equally, whether royalty or the tea lady.

Some of Bobby's great stories at that memorable dinner had echoes of Peter Beardsley's style, particularly when remembering the antics of former player Paul Gascoigne, known to all as Gazza.

One of the best recalled a tour to Australia when, at breakfast, the waiter asked Gazza what he would like.

"I just fancy a bacon sandwich," he said.

A couple of minutes passed and the waiter returned looking apologetic.

"I'm terribly sorry, sir, but the kitchen is completely out of bacon."

Only Gazza could reply, "You've got a country full of sheep and no bacon!"

Bobby and friends wondered if a Gazza wit was developing. It wasn't.

It was like the time when Bobby saw him, unusually, in deep concentration and clearly trying to work out a difficult problem.

"What's on your mind, son?"

"It's me sister boss."

"What about her?"

"Well, she has two brothers but I only have one."

Right.

With memories of that famous Courtney Walsh dinner years back, John was enjoying hosting a crop of cricket events and thoroughly enjoying a sport which has grown like Topsy around the world but remains peculiarly English.

Even though it has now gained a toe-hold across the Atlantic, many Americans struggled to understand a game which could go on for five days – and still end in a draw.

They also failed to grasp why a full day could be spent sheltering from the rain and having long discussions about whether it was going to stop or not.

For all its faults, cricket still maintained a special atmosphere where fans of opposing counties or nations could sit side by side and never dream of the yobbish violence which still sometimes reared its ugly head at football grounds.

One of John's best trips came in 2010 when he was invited to speak in Australia alongside the games against England.

The luxury life continued as he made the trip in sponsor Etihad's first-class cabin. When you are a young backpacker, a 24-hour flight in economy might be endurable, but he had become well used to turning left on planes.

A comfortable trip to Abu Dhabi, then a short stopover in their executive lounge including a relaxing massage, and he felt like a spring lamb when he landed in Sydney.

One of the best parts of the trip came in beautiful Hobart in Tasmania where John was due to be guest speaker at the lunch for Lord's Taverners, the very successful cricket and show business charity which did excellent work for disadvantaged youngsters.

John loved compering his talk-ins, and, the evening before, he had been at the local Wrest Point Hotel where the star attractions were recent Australian captain Ricky Pointing and Shane Warne, probably one of the best spin bowlers ever.

Shane's name was all over the front pages of the papers as well as the sports pages at the back.

Australia were not doing well against the old enemy and many of their supporters reckoned that Shane should come out of retirement and work his magic again.

The front pages were full of regular updates on Shane's relationship with big name actress Liz Hurley.

The function room at Wrest Point is huge and perfectly designed for an event like this one.

From the wide stage at the front the tiered audience rose steeply so that everyone in the thousand-strong congregation had a perfect view.

After the chat on stage, the regular routine of inviting questions from the floor was in full swing.

John loved the fine style of the Australian male delivering a well-considered question which would get straight to the point.

One chap raised his hand, soon had the mic, and rose to his feet steadily, needed only the wide hat with dangling corks to complete the look.

"Look here Shane," he began and soon got to the point.

"You should be back on the field hammering the Poms, not flying off to London to have it off with that Liz Hurley!"

The Oz version of "Here, here" rang round the huge auditorium.

In similar fashion, Shane rose to his feet, paused and

delivered a short and sharp response.

"What would you rather do mate?"

Question man, still holding his mic, was straight back with an even shorter response.

"Good point, Shane."

The audience appeared to concur and that was that. Perhaps our politicians could listen and learn and trim the length of their long-winded rambling debates too.

The game itself, after these highly successful warm-up events, was special too.

After the lunch where John spoke, guests made the short walk to the ferry which took them on the short hop to the game, a fast and furious one day international which started in glorious sunshine and ended under floodlights.

Abrasive wit was much in evidence in the crowd, but there was friendliness there rather than malice.

At one point, a fast ball from an England seamer smacked into the helmet of an Australian batsmen and he flopped down in some pain.

An Australian supporter soon gave his opinion.

"You dirty English bastard."

Each "a" in the second word was elongated to make it even more effective.

John's host was Paul who had organised the lunch and he was soon on the defensive on behalf of his honoured guest from England.

"Do you mind, mate; my guest here is an English bastard."

In a kind of conciliation, back came the reply.

"No offence, English bastard, can I get you a cold

beer?"

Ah, top level international diplomacy lives on.

For all the good humour that was around, John also saw some of the outrageous behaviour which gave celebrities a hard time.

He remembered well a very happy tour of talk-ins with (now Sir) Ian Botham.

After a career of stellar success in county and international cricket, he had come to Durham County Cricket Club to end his career, and John was booked to host the series of ten events at the pubs and clubs of Scottish and Newcastle Breweries, the County's main sponsor.

They all went like a storm, and venues which would usually be quiet on a weekday evening were packed out with the famous Beefy on the bill.

After one event, some excellent post-event networking was flowing nicely, and Ian had a splendid surprise when an old playing colleague came all the way from deepest Hampshire to see him.

They were having a great time, leaning on the bar with pint glasses in hand, sharing great memories of people and places.

Out of the blue, a man who had been at the event marched towards them and, without an "excuse me" or a word of introduction, thrust a cricket programme just about at Ian's nose.

"Here, put your autograph on this. It's for my son 'cos I think you're shite."

Some people might have been inclined to deck the bad-mannered creature but, to his eternal credit, Ian smiled, signed it and said, "Ah well, one out of two isn't bad."

He turned back to his old pal and ignored the yobbish interruption.

On another evening, John was enjoying a pleasant dinner with Ian and the senior brewery management to chat through some future events.

The England physiotherapist was in the patch and came along to join them.

Ian was on good form and enjoying multiple pints of bitter during the meal.

The physio, always ready to offer good advice, turned his attention to Ian.

"You are lucky you know. While you are running around playing cricket for several hours most days, you'll just burn off the mega-calories in beer. Once you retire though, if you keep up that level of consumption, you'll end up like Porky Pig."

"I love you too, "said Ian. "But seriously, what am I supposed to do? I'm a social animal."

"Well, how about switching to a dry white wine?"

"Fair enough doc, I'll give it a go."

The host from S&N caught the eye of the waiter to order a fresh round.

"So Ian, the start of a new healthy life. What would you like?"

"A pint of Chardonnay would be good."

He'd heard half of the advice then.

Ian's life was not all plain sailing, but, like the incident with the bad-mannered guy with the programme, he'd learned how to largely stay away from trouble, mainly by not being in places where it might happen.

It was not that easy for some other big names and lessons were not always learned.

When you were young, rich and recognised everywhere you went, it was easy to mess up on the self-discipline and waste the chance of a good career and a huge income.

Not that long ago, even very good footballers would end their careers with not very much in the bank and considered themselves to have done well if they ran a pub or a newsagent's shop in their retirement.

One guy always stuck in John's mind. His old friend Kenny Johnson had played for little Hartlepool United from the late Fifties onwards and scored goal after goal. Admittedly, this was not at top level, but everyone who saw him reckoned that he could score goals against anyone.

In the modern game, Kenny would have been worth millions and would have earned a huge salary instead of being happy making a success from his fish and chip shop he bought when his playing days were over.

Ken always carried one of his old playing contracts which was a great talking point.

He earned ten pounds a week, and seven pounds in the summer during the close season when no matches were played.

After one annual pay round, Kenny complained to the boss that another player was getting eight pounds in the summer compared to his own seven.

"With respect Ken, he's a rather better player than you."

Kenny's reply went into legend, "Not in the summer,

he's not."

What really put the icing on this contract from an age now gone was the stipulation that:

"If a player contracted to the club desires to step out with a young lady, she must be presented to the Board of Directors so that they may judge is she is deemed to be suitable."

Then again, that clause in some modern players' contracts might save a heap of trouble.

In the modern world, the problem for many young players in a range of sports is that they enjoy the fame but don't know how to handle their new place in life.

History is littered with tales like the footballers from Leeds United who ended up in serious trouble in their own city centre.

Of course, it's hard to give up on being young and be professional and, again, it was Kevin Keegan who summed it up best.

One of his young players was in bother for drinking in a night club in the early hours when he should have been tucked up in bed before an important game.

Kevin called in him to his office and kept the advice short and to the point. "You can do well son. Don't do this again or you are gone. Work hard for a few years and you can buy a bloody night club if you want one."

Sometimes that kind of advice hit the spot and worked; sometimes it seemed to and didn't.

John heard the story of a young cricketer who was looking set for a very successful and, these days, very lucrative career.

The days had gone when top England players would

be seeking an ordinary job to pay the bills when they stopped playing in their mid-thirties or so.

Many went on to well paid jobs in the media, and, as their careers peaked, some could earn millions for a few weeks of cricket in the Indian Premier League and the like.

John had heard the story of one young cricketer in the south who, with a career well on the rise, had been sent home for being caught drinking in the early hours on a young England players' international tour despite a final warning.

His well-respected coach, with long experience at the top level of the game, called him in to his office on his return.

He was expecting a two-hour rollicking, but it was nearly two hours shorter.

"In twenty years from now, someone will recognise you and say one of two things. They might point you out and describe you as one of the best players who ever wore an England cricket shirt.

Or they might describe you as a hopeless drunk who threw away every chance he was given. Now get out of my sight and decide which one it is to be."

The young man's career went from strength to strength and all seemed well, until he hit the self-destruct button again in a late-night brawl in a seedy night club.

At that time of night, there'll always be some local drunk who thinks he can make a name for himself by thumping the big star in front of him.

The sensible thing to do for the big name is to never to be in a place where that can happen. Sadly, sense doesn't always win – even when a few stupid moments can cost millions, a reputation, and a future.

Then again, very few of us do the sensible thing every time.

Some lucky people can make a torrent of mistakes and never seem to be hit by the consequences they deserve.

Or perhaps it's just a matter of time.

John's taste in reading matter had widened, and he found himself marvelling at what Shakespeare really wrote and what, in his world, "tragedy" really meant.

It was not the modern meaning of something sad or heart-breaking, but a very old dramatic structure which meant that a man's faults would always be the cause of his undoing.

John had seen enough of big sporting names at close quarters to know that some of them had characters which almost invited a tragic end in the Shakespearian sense, and he was convinced that nothing could surprise him anymore.

A few weeks later, he would have the biggest surprise of his life.

CHAPTER 12 – MAKING IT FIRM

There's a lovely line in *The Boxer*, one of Simon and Garfunkel's best songs – "a pocketful of mumbles, such are promises."

In life, and especially the speaking circuit, John had learned the truth of that, but, lately, more promises were coming good than falling flat.

He had learned the importance of making conversations firm and getting them in writing, either personally, or through his agent.

The ambition of people in the early hours after a substantial drink could be a lot stronger than that they could deliver in reality.

Sometime, a guest at a dinner would watch proceedings and think how easy it all was.

You simply booked a date, a venue and a speaker – then watched the money roll in.

If only. The bit they often forgot was organising several hundred people to attend and spend their money.

If John accepted a booking on a handshake and put it in his diary months ahead, it would be a prize nuisance if it failed to materialise and a date which could have been an earner was sacrificed.

At a well-meaning discussion in a late night post-function bar, John would make sure that he had the intended client's email address and promise to contact him next day – which he did without fail.

He would offer thanks for the enquiry and set out his terms which included a 20% non-refundable deposit to secure the date.

This would often bear fruit, but sometimes, in the cold and sober light of day, the cheery chap from the bar would plead poverty – "but it's definitely going ahead."

John's reply was to say that there was no problem, and he'd release the date until he'd had another contact from him with a definite booking.

That left an honourable solution, and, usually, further contact was there none.

Occasionally, John did get an unexpected result. One evening he compered a particularly successful evening in Manchester with two very good guests – a sportsman and a well-known Sky Sports broadcaster.

The audience loved it and it made a serious profit for the organiser.

In the melee afterwards a chap came for a chat. He had loved the event and wanted to put it on at his own venue.

John detected a most definite north east accent and asked where the proposed do would take place.

"You might not know it" he said, "It's the Old Comrades' Club in Seaham in County Durham."

John did know it.

"I have been there, but, unless it's grown a lot, it only holds about a hundred people doesn't it?"

"That's the one. And we'll put on a great night."

"We'd love to do it" said John, "but, and with maximum respect, for the three of us it won't be cheap."

"How much?"

John told him and waited for his eyes to water. They didn't.

Did they have a date in mind?

Mr Hopeful did indeed. It was some months away and on his birthday, so he'd love it to happen then.

John had the usual feeling that splendid wine-fuelled intentions would not turn solid, so he tried another tactic he'd learned.

"The only thing is that, as a new client, the guys would need full payment up front. Give me an email address and I'll get my lady to sort you an invoice and we'll get it all sorted."

That would kill it.

It didn't.

"Give me a minute" said the prospect and wandered off towards what was presumably the direction of his hotel room upstairs.

He returned carrying a tatty holdall, guided John to a table in a private corner and proceeded to count out the loot in full.

Just goes to show that the unexpected can happen.

The evening went ahead and it was indeed a great success with the hundred-strong audience making up for their small numbers with massive enthusiasm.

Even the auction, which John conducted, was quite a success; there was clearly some money in the room.

They had managed to acquire an Alan Shearer signed shirt – especially collectable as his playing career had recently ended.

The bidding went up to an unforeseen £5,000 and the successful buyer was clearly chuffed to bits.

"Well played mate, "said John, "have a word with Bob the club treasurer and he'll fix a trip to see you to hand over the shirt and settle up."

With echoes of the night the event was booked, he announced that there was no need for that, reached into his back pocket and then peeled off the five grand in big notes.

At the end of the evening, John was winding up and giving thanks to all, internally amazed that, despite the large fee for such a small gathering, the night would be in profit.

"I've done some biggies over the years, but I've never seen such generous cash bidders. This must be the centre of the black economy in the north of England."

By the way they all looked at their shoes, it clearly was.

CHAPTER 13 – WOMAN, I CAN HARDLY EXPLAIN

Another booking which came good was the offer to speak in Corfu which came from the millionaire at the Civil Engineers' dinner who'd also launched John on the cruise ship circuit.

In fact, it came good twice. The Greek chap, Nikos, had two prospects. One was for John to fly over for a few days to speak at a private dinner at the hotel for a key client, then to return later in the summer to speak at a couple of events and tag on a couple of weeks' holiday as their guests.

John chatted it over with Janet and, as she had some potential family commitments on the first of the dates, she suggested that John did the first trip solo and she'd love to come for the second visit with the holiday.

John had some memories of the Greek islands from younger days when he and Janet would do it on a cheap and cheerful basis, live simply and soak up the sunshine.

This trip was in a totally different league.

John had a short and comfortable direct flight from Newcastle to Corfu, and the fragrant warmth greeted him as soon as he stepped off the plane.

As promised his base was to be the Marbella Corfu Hotel and if it was as good as the website, it would be something special.

Fran, from the management team at the hotel, met him personally off his flight, and a nice car took them on the short trip past gorgeous green countryside with glimpses of a sparkling blue sea.

This was a great way to start a Wednesday afternoon – a day which had started only a few hours before in a damp and grey Newcastle.

Fran's easy smile and natural charm was accompanied by a genuinely warm welcome to the hotel.

His cases were whisked off to his room by a porter and he enjoyed a refreshing cool fruit juice.

"Why don't you have a couple of hours' break in your room?" suggested Fran, "and then we can have a bite of dinner about eight and talk you through plans for Friday."

"Room" was an understatement. It was a beautiful suite with a huge terrace complete with a hot tub, which John thought might work equally well as a cold tub given the rising temperatures.

He leaned on the white stone balustrade and took in the spectacular view which spanned the hotel itself down the slope of the hillside, and across to the wide view of the sea which stretched to the horizon.

Over a fine dinner dominated by fresh local produce and wine, Fran introduced John to the hotel manager Telemachos and the three of them laughed a lot as well as taking in a smidge of organisational discussion.

"Nikos is flying in first thing tomorrow," they explained.

"The four of us can have lunch, and he'll tell you more about the client."

John picked up that this was special. The company was in petrochemicals and operated worldwide with one base here in Greece.

Nikos was a key partner and had fixed the dinner on the forthcoming Friday to cement the relationship and look after them well.

The dinner on Friday would be for just fifty key people, with John as keynote speaker.

Speaking to a small audience can be harder than to a crowd of over a thousand in a big hotel venue, but John had been around long enough now to know that he could make it work.

His smallest ever group was in the boardroom of a merchant banking company on the Isle of Man and that had worked like a dream – especially as one of the twelve-strong audience was a Government Minister.

"They are nice people" said Telemachos," and I've met them a few times now. Their boss is a multi-millionaire and sharp as a tack. They won't be here until late Friday afternoon, but you can get to know them during the evening."

The planning evening felt much more like a fun night with friends than a business meeting and soon it was midnight.

"You must try a special ouzo as your nightcap," said Telemachos, the perfect host.

Holding his hands up defensively he said, "You mentioned that you'd been around the Greek islands as a young man, and I'm sure you tried some very average tourist ouzo. This is the best."

And it was, and then some.

John walked back up the stone stairs to his suite. The lights around the gardens had been dimmed, and the whole view was beyond improvement: unfeasibly bright stars against a soft velvet backdrop and a shiny sea reflecting the huge moon.

These guys could run master classes in hospitality and they topped it as he headed for bed.

Among many other things, they had talked music over dinner and discovered a joint passion for Bob Dylan.

As John walked through the door of his perfect accommodation for the night, he discovered that someone had set the in-room hi fi to the gentle strains of a Dylan album.

On the table was a long wooden box. It was packed with straw and held a bottle of the top-end ouzo which he'd enjoyed at the end of dinner.

The accompanying card was perfect;

"We are delighted to have you here John. Please enjoy this ouzo at home and remember us here at Marbella Corfu."

My word, this beat a chocolate on the pillow, though those were there as well.

There was another note beside the most welcome gift.

"Have a leisurely breakfast John and then meet us and Nikos in reception at 12.30. We're heading off for a very relaxed lunch – dress code is very informal – shorts and sandals. Ties banned." Telemachos and Fran. Xx

John eventually nodded off with a smile on his face, lulled to sleep by the gentle sound of the sea down the hill.

Thursday came and he felt strange as, for the first time in his life, he dressed for a business meeting in shorts, sandals, and a floppy polo shirt.

The oddness disappeared when he arrived in reception and found that the other three had done the same – including Nikos, who greeted him with a huge bear hug and a smiling "kali mera" of a Greek good morning.

"Off we go" said Telemachos" I'm your driver."

He led them outside and down the hill to a jetty where a splendid powerboat stood, emblazoned with the hotel name.

With him in the driver's berth, John sat between Fran and Nikos behind him and was told that the trip would take about twenty minutes and they would dine on the beach.

The boat skipped above the water, and Fran leaned forward to lift a hatch which revealed a fridge containing champagne and canapes.

Was there anything these guys couldn't do?

The lunch was at a restaurant which was indeed, literally, on the beach and only served fresh seafood – fresh, as in landed today.

John was in heaven as a seafood fan, especially with the calamari which could taste like rubber at home but melted in the mouth here.

Kali mera, calamari.

In yet another perfect atmosphere, Nikos briefed John on the client and the key players and his hopes for the night.

"We just want you to do what you do well John. Get them smiling, make them feel good and like they belong here."

The plan was to include cocktails on the terrace, a gourmet dinner, and a little surprise afterwards.

On the Friday evening, the dress code was a total contrast to the planning lunch on the beach.

The gentlemen wore immaculate dinner suits and the ladies looked gorgeous in what were clearly exquisite designer creations.

Even though there were only the promised fifty or so people there, the pre-dinner drinks went by in whirl.

John tried to remember who was who, and was particularly struck by one pair of key players who looked very in control and had a sharp sense of humour.

He wore a clearly expensive dinner suit and she had a black lace dress studded with pearls.

They were clearly part of a team and the other guests, judging by the body language, saw the two of them as being leaders of the pack.

John guessed Managing Director and Personal Assistant, and it turned out he was right.

The woman was like nobody he'd met before. She squeezed his arm, wished him all the best and he thought he felt a genuine, not figurative, spark of electricity from her.

He tried not to, but couldn't, be caught by her piercing blue eyes. She was blonde, attractive but not classically beautiful, and was charisma on legs.

As the time rolled round for his speech, John was busy with his own mental preparation which nobody else would understand.

He remembered well the first time he'd spoken to a monster audience in Park Lane in the Great Room at Grosvenor House.

That place can be daunting or inspiring and John chose the second alternative.

He remembered still the debate going on inside his head as the moment to perform approached.

One little man in his brain told him to be nervous and that he was going to make a mess of it.

A much bigger internal opponent listed the positives. Between London and Park Lane there were millions of people and they had invited him. Above all, this was a great chance to show a big and influential audience just how good he was. It was a chance to shine.

Nikos introduced John to the audience and told them how good he was and that they were delighted that he had made the trip from England to be with them tonight.

John's self-delivered mental pep talk worked perfectly and he had them from hello.

As he always did, he spread his gaze around the room as he spoke to make them all feel involved, but he kept catching the eye of the blonde lady from charisma central.

She was rocking with laughter in all the right places and her approval seemed to lift John's performance to an even higher level. He had done his homework, and carefully wove in the key lines which Nikos wanted to hear about future collaborations with this huge global company.

When he finished, to a round of applause which sounded more like a big theatre than a private dining room for fifty people, it was clear that mission was accomplished.

The audience loved him and Nikos had clearly received the perfect foundation.

Amid a real buzz, John felt as if he had a receiving line of compliment makers a bit like a royal greeting guests.

His blonde lady was the first across and she stayed at

his side to hear the stream of praise as though she belonged there.

Out of the corner of his eye, John saw the man whom he took to be the MD in urgent conversation and it looked as if something was adrift.

He scurried across to John's blonde companion and whispered urgently.

"The surprise is scuppered" she said. "Our late-night guest has slipped on the stone staircase and broken his wrist. He's on the way to hospital."

"There's always a plan B" said John, though she clearly didn't believe him.

"Come and look" she said, leading him to a side door just off their dining room.

The room was beautifully set out like a very high-quality cabaret club. About a dozen tables for four looked perfect with flowers and candles, and the main lighting was gently dimmed.

The tables were arranged in a semi-circle with the focus on a small and slightly raised stage. The stage contained a nice guitar on its stand and two microphones, one for a vocalist and one lower down for the guitar.

There was also some sophisticated-looking sound equipment which a glum-looking techie chap was leaning on – but no guitarist.

"The plan was" said Barbara, for he had finally discovered her name, "to end with some gentle music to make the evening perfect."

"Told you there was a plan B," said John, "I'll do it."

"Oh do piss off," said Barbara.

"How was the motivation course – did you enjoy all of it?" asked John, and that set her giggling.

"I can do it, I promise. I cut my teeth in folk clubs and the like and I won't let you down. I still keep my hand in. Go and delay the guests for ten minutes while I run through a few things with the techie guy and we'll be fine."

"You don't want to let your boss down, do you Barbara?"

"Which boss?" asked Barbara.

"The guy with the designer dinner suit who's been attached to you like a limpet all night."

There seemed to be almost a tinge of jealousy there which John hadn't intended, perhaps.

"Tim's my personal assistant, you daft git. Why do people still presume that the woman is always the number two? He's a good PA, but I'm his boss. I own 80% of the company."

"I have had a bit of a rough time lately, mainly a few business headaches. Tim's a good guy who would walk through walls for me – but that's it, there's no romance there."

John hadn't asked to be told that, but Barbara clearly thought that it needed to be said.

"Now you get the guitar sorted and I'll head off the posse for ten minutes."

Come out and tell me when you are ready and sit with me in the audience before we introduce you.

The normally self-assured John stood there simultaneously blushing, glazed over and mesmerised before he shook himself into action.

John went through a mini-sound check and, with the help of a very good reverb set-up and the rest, he was sounding good.

He went back to the main room to find Barbara and Nikos in deep conversation and all looked very well.

John whispered in Barbara's ear and could almost taste her.

"All set up boss, and I'm sorry I thought you were the gopher."

"No problem, I like it that you liked me before you knew I was a bloody multi-millionaire – it can be a nuisance honest."

"How did you know I liked you?"

"I know things."

And she did.

The congregation, happily delayed by extra supplies of cool champagne, filed through to the room next door and just about cooed in admiration.

Barbara headed for the stage and the techie guy made her look even better with a soft spotlight.

"We've had a wonderful evening, and it's not over yet. We promised you a surprise after dinner, and I've had a couple too. John could feel her eyes on him and it was about more than the guitar."

"May I thank everyone here at this magical hotel for looking after us so well, and to John Bremner for showing us why he's one of the most in-demand speakers around."

A well-deserved double round of applause filled the room.

"I now have two introductions to make. The first is to

welcome our host tonight who is now our new main board director – Nikos Spyros.

This clearly was a major bolt from the blue, but Nikos had a top reputation and the standing ovation sealed the deal.

"You will see the stage behind me is all set for some musical entertainment and those of you who like detective novels will have spotted that there is a certain something missing."

"Some of you know that the flashing blue lights a little earlier were for our guest guitarist who is now comfortable in hospital with his broken wrist which came about after colliding with a stone staircase.

We've just heard from his manager who sends his apologies and the news that his client won't be playing a guitar for a while."

"As you all know, there are no problems, only opportunities.

Will you please welcome our superstar guitar vocalist – Mr John Bremner."

The audience didn't know if this was an elaborate gag, but doubts were soon dispelled.

John walked calmly to the stage, sat on the bar stool and started a gentle finger-picking guitar introduction which showed that he knew what he was doing.

"This is a new one for me. I don't do audiences for my music, but I love playing and singing for friends. And that's who I'm with tonight."

When the applause faded away, he kept the introduction going and talked over it like an old pro.

"We had dinner here a little earlier this week and I

know that we have some Bob Dylan fans in the audience – do we have a few more?"

The response came in the positive.

Mr Dylan has been around for over fifty years, but clearly the younger people in the audience were fans too.

"Just to show I'm down there with the kids," smiled John, "I'm up with the times too. Do we have Adele fans in the room?"

We certainly did.

Still keeping the hypnotic guitar pick going, John introduced his first song as though he'd been doing it for ever.

"Adele had a monster hit with this song not long back, but only a tiny number of people know that Dylan wrote it. He doesn't just do the rock and protest songs – he does perfect tenderness too. This is - *Make You Feel My Love*."

"It's for Dylan fans, Adele fans, and anyone who's had a tough time lately."

As planned, the techie dimmed the room lights a notch down, and a single overhead spotlight picked out John.

He flowed seamlessly into the first verse:

When the rain is blowing in your face

And the whole world is on your case

I can offer you a warm embrace

To make you feel my love."

The audience was almost in darkness, but John could see Barbara's eyes and some stray light bouncing from the spotlight made it look as if they were filling up.

They were.

He finished the song with an instrumental flourish and Barbara led the genuine applause – or perhaps if the boss liked it, they thought they all should.

"Wow" said John, "I'll have to think of another one now.

Let's do one you will all know and you are most welcome to join in the chorus."

He gently launched into Leonard Cohen's Hallelujah and, as he said in his seamless yet unrehearsed introduction, as well as being a classic in its own right it had received various resurrections, if you'll pardon the pun, as a film soundtrack, a multitude of cover versions, and a soulful version by Alexandra Burke on Opportunity Knocks, or whatever the latest talent show incarnation is called.

It's a funny thing, but fifty amateur but keen singers do often produce a pleasant harmony, and few present would ever forget the night they were part of a beautiful sound, with the starry sky outside their window.

John surprised himself with what he, and his fingers, remembered. He had done some work with Alzheimer's Charities, partly because his dad been through it, and many experts had told him that the memory required to sing a song or play an instrument often lasted much longer than other fields of memory.

John had often visited Sunderland Royal Hospital just up the road from home.

It had a world-leading Alzheimer's and Dementia Department and the staff themselves had created something extraordinary.

Knowing that sitting in a dull ward all day can hinder

progress, they had established the Alexandra Suite, a kind of social club for their dementia patients and it really worked.

John had dropped in a few times and found it inspiring – despite once coming fourth in the musical memories quiz.

He also discovered that remembering gags lasted a long time too. Patients who found full sentences sometimes difficult could recite a favourite gag and not drop a stitch.

John meandered through some of his limited back catalogue which heavily featured musical youth including the Beatles and the Animals, and it continued to go well.

"Time for the last one" said John, 'cos the pie and peas are due."

They audience shouted "no" and sounded as if they meant it.

"Yet another surprise," said John, "our techie lad tonight has been brilliant, so let's hear it for him."

After the applause died down, John said, "Better than that he's got pedigree. He's living and working here in Greece these days, but Danny is from South Shields, in the north east."

"Better yet, he plays harmonica, and we did a ninety second rehearsal of one of my favourite songs ever. This will sound great or garbage – no pressure, Danny - but none of you succeeded in life without taking risks, so here goes. "

"A big hit for north east band Lindisfarne this was. And it won a Novello award for lovely Rod Clements who wrote it. This is *Meet Me on the Corner* ...."

If you know the song, it kicks off with a driving harmonica intro and the two of them, particularly Danny, nailed it.

As well as being a crowd pleaser, it had some depth too, including the lines which had been lodged in John's head for decades:

Lay down your bundles of rags and reminders

And lay your wares on the ground ....

John finished, drew another generous round of applause for Danny, who blushed to his roots, and flopped into an empty chair which Barbara had kept for him by her side.

She hugged him and kissed him, saying "Give me a second" as she went up the mic.

"Thank you so, so much John. We'd heard that you'd be a star as our speaker, but who could have imagined that brilliant musical performance. And here's my Geordie accent – you were lush marra."

"Two more things we'd like you do for us John. Please come and do that again for us at our New Year's Eve Party – it's at the Burj al Arab in Dubai if you fancy it.

And we'd love you to spread your presentation skills around our company."

"But that's enough of work – let's party."

A party did continue as Barbara and John talked and talked.

John had only heard about it in films before, but the people around them melted away.

Barbara leaned close to him and said, "Confession time. You've been on our radar for some time now. Nikos, as well as being an old friend, is one of our top talent spotters.

He raved about you after that first time he saw you in England and we've been watching you ever since."

"Watching me?"

"Yes, we've been keeping tabs. Nikos usually gets it right. A few of my key leadership team are there because one of our associates followed a hunch and recommended someone to me.

I feel as if I know you well already, especially with my video library of you. A few times when a techie team have been putting you on big screen at conferences and the like, they've also done a recording for us too."

"Bloody hell, that's sneaky."

"Nah, it's using technology for effectiveness. We didn't become one of the biggest petrochemical companies in the world by not using what's out there. When we need to, we can spend big to earn big.

We use everything from surveillance agencies to friends in governments around the world. Top people rate us because we can deliver. We take calculated risks when we need to, but rarely take risks on people. They're our biggest asset, so we get them right.

And it works – we have you here and loving it."

"True."

"I know a lot about you, down to your shoes size. Size nine, regular fitting. And you use contact lenses on stage; one for long vision, one for short, and they have correction for astigmatism.

We've checked you out, just a few bits to go, and everyone who knows you rates you highly. You are also dependable and don't let people down."

"I feel as if Special Branch have been through my files."

"Yes, they've been helpful too."

She was joking, surely?

John felt a bit like a specimen in a laboratory, but also intrigued by this woman and this organisation who had spotted something special in him.

It felt good to be honest.

"I feel even better now that I've seen you in the flesh. When are you due to fly back John?"

"It's booked for tomorrow afternoon."

"Could you stay till Monday and we can have a proper chat over the weekend?"

"I'd love to if I can change the flight."

"Consider it sorted."

And they went back into their private world for another hour.

CHAPTER 14 – THE FOUND WEEKEND

Now that John's later flight was, in Barbara's word, "sorted", she could almost relax, but she had a "to do" list in her head.

"Before I forget" she said, "what you do call twenty Cockneys in a filing cabinet?"

John, genuinely, had on idea.

"Sorted" she giggled, "new one for your repertoire."

"Tim's going to interrupt us shortly. He does look after me, and he's going to tell me that I need a few hours' sleep before a conference call at six in the morning."

"Who the hell is up at six on a Sunday morning?"

"People in Dubai. It's a working day for them and I need to talk to the chairman of a company we might be buying."

"Might?"

"He wants nearly two hundred million dollars equivalent and I've offered one hundred and fifty – we'll see."

"Bloody hell."

"Let's leave that. We'll have lunch tomorrow. I'll get Tim to draw up a consultancy contract for you to help us. There's five minutes to block out; if you like it, then we can talk."

"Do you know John, I'm usually the most logical person in the world, but I need to turn my edit switch off. Let me tell you two things and you can smile or tell me to piss off. First one is that I'm sure we met in a former life.

I know that's sheer bollocks, but it's what I feel. And secondly, I feel electricity when you come near me. There you go – two choices."

John smiled and she smiled back.

"And that Dylan and Adele song you sang just for me. It wrecked me, but in a good way."

"Good, it was meant to."

"And there's another song – you didn't do it – but it's rattling around my head. Do you know *Perfect Day* – the Lou Reed one? That's just what today's felt like.

Here I am, the hard-headed tough nut business woman, and you've got me like a submissive young girl."

"I wish."

If there was electricity before, there was nuclear fission now.

Can you have an erotic silence? Yes, you can, and this was one.

John filled it.

"Do you know that the song was allegedly written about spending a perfect day wrecked on cocaine? I thought it was bloody hilarious when the BBC did that production number on the song with loads of worthy singers – recording a hymn of praise to hard drugs"

"You're making that up."

"I'm not."

And he wasn't.

"And another thing. That Lindisfarne song you did; I've known it forever and love it, but I'm just getting the rags and reminders bit."

"Great, me too. It's brilliant isn't it. How the hell do you write lines as good as that? In the end, that's all there is really.

You can wear expensive designer clothes but they all end up as rags, and it's the reminders of the special things in life which are the really priceless things."

"Anyway, tell me about you Barbara – I want to know."

"It's pretty simple really. My dad died when I was only nine and my mum brought me up. She's my hero and I still talk to her every day.

She still lives in Manchester where I grew up, but I was chuffed to bits when I could buy her a lovely house where she'd be safe for ever. My dad would have been so happy.

I think what's driven me is wanting to look after my mum the way my dad would have wanted to. I started out as a bloody office junior in the company I now just about own.

I kept seeing people cock things up and thinking that I could do better. And I did. That's about all there is really.

I have an apartment in London where I live most of the time when I'm in England, but she wants to stay where she feels at home."

"I get that" said John.

"Do you know what John? You've never even hinted that you want to get me into bed, and, this time of night, you'd be amazed how many unlikely creatures make the offer."

"I'd be letting myself down if I did. Call me a soppy git if you like, but I feel like I'm walking into something special, and I'm terrified of spoiling it. I keep hearing songs too like I never got them before. You know *The*

First Time Ever I Saw Your Face?

Like the beating heart of a captive bird? Call me a double soppy git if you like, but that's how it feels. I thought I was hard-headed too, but I'm well out of my depth. I don't want to get it all wrong."

"You're getting it absolutely right."

"Here's Tim right on cue."

"Sorry boss, but you told me to order you to bed, to be sharp for our conference call at six."

"You're right Tim, and I'll need a few minutes in the morning for you to draft John's contract with us. "

"John, lunch is too far away. Shall we say brunch at eleven? Please?"

Barbara kissed John goodnight, and he could still feel her touch as he walked to bed in a daze.

He slept on and off – deeply when he did, and wide awake when he didn't. Had tonight really happened? Yes, it had, but what to do next?

CHAPTER 15 – LADIES WHO BRUNCH

Despite the late night, John was showered and presentable by eight and on his third coffee while he tidied his room and cleared out the junk Sunday morning emails.

Well, mainly junk. There was a brief business one from Tim asking for John's bank details for payments and the contact emails for his accountant and legal guy.

They were soon answered – this was all feeling real.

Better still, there was a short but very sweet one from Barbara which was sent at 5.45 am – obviously just before her vital conference call.

"A few hours' sleep but I've woken up feeling like a spring lamb – your effect. ☺ Conference call shouldn't take long but I might have a nap afterwards. Really looking forward to seeing you for brunch at eleven. Why don't you come to me to save us getting a crop of interruptions in the restaurant? It's suite six, top floor."

Then she'd either fallen asleep with her finger on the x key or she'd sent a string of kisses. Barbara wouldn't fall asleep unless she wanted to.

John had several tries at composing a reply and deleted a few attempts which sounded horribly cheesy and is if written by a lovesick teenager.

He eventually settled on:

"Can't wait till eleven – really look forward to being together again. Trust your conference call goes well. It will. Suite six it is."

He added his own string of kisses and wondered if there were etiquette rules about making the number more or less than Barbara's total.

John felt like a kid on Christmas Eve when the clock seemed to refuse to move forward.

At ten, he went for a walk around the lovely hotel grounds and came back and tidied his room again.

Eventually the clock took pity and it was almost eleven. He pondered whether to be there early or to be fashionably five minutes later.

In the end, he rang the door-bell on suite six at exactly eleven.

She looked the same but totally different; the designer dress replaced by tight blue denim jeans and white lacy top, and clearly no bra.

For a master of words, John could only come up with, "You look great and .." She ended the Shakespearian quality sonnet with a kiss which lasted.

She led him by the hand to the terrace which was like his but even bigger, but with the same knockout view across to the sea.

The table had been beautifully set with a range of tempting food and, at the centre, a huge ice bucket holding bottles of fresh orange juice and champagne.

"Are we celebrating?" John asked.

"Hell yes. I've got you to myself. Start with a mimosa? I'm in the States too much; I mean a buck's fizz."

"Sounds perfect. You are too kind young lady; I meant your conference call."

"Oh, that was fine. You remember he wanted two hundred million and I offered one fifty? He was probably expecting me to meet him half way at one seven five."

"Is that what happened then?"

"Nah. I knocked him onto the back foot a bit. I told

him we were probably looking elsewhere, but we could now go up to one forty and no higher."

"He said there was no chance."

"So that one's all over then?"

She giggled in a way which he found a turn-on.

"He accepted my original bid of one fifty."

"God, you're good. "

"I know. We both do that, don't we? Believe in ourselves I mean."

"Spot on. If you don't think of yourself as the best, how can you expect other people to rate you?

So, is your deal all done and dusted? Talk me through it; you know what I do, and I really want to understand what you do.

Don't you feel nervous about committing one hundred and fifty million dollars?"

"Well, it's not committed yet. Tim, bless him, he's been in touch with our finance and legal guys in the middle of the night. We have an option agreement, but we can walk away without paying a penny if we want to."

"Why would you want to?"

"I also have an offer in for another company covering that region – currently held at $160 million on option. We're expanding what we do in petrochemicals in the Middle East and beyond.

It works better to buy a good outfit which is already set up there and doing well, rather than starting from scratch ourselves.

Whatever works out, we won't even change the name of the company we'll own: they both have good reputations and we can build on that and keep a solid supply and customer base."

"You obviously know this inside out and you're good with words you know; I got all of that. But why have the trouble of two sets of negotiations going on instead of settling on one?"

"Thank you, kind sir, – not as good with words as you though.

The two alternatives thing is something I've always done in life – plan B in case plan A gets stuck."

"So, if you are going to end up only buying one company and dropping the other one, won't you feel a bit guilty about letting one of them down?"

"No, that's business I guess. We've used our contacts to make sure that they both know that they are in a beauty contest. It's the way of the world isn't it – I'm sure that there have been times when you have been in the frame for a big event with somebody else competing. I bet you win more than you lose, but it comes with the territory, doesn't it?"

"By the way, talking of Tim who should be sleeping like a log after working all night, I trust your little ears were burning while you slept; Tim spent about an hour of his time on your case."

"My case?"

"Yes" she giggled again, "Despite all our homework so far, our corporate governance guys insist on doing a full risk assessment on any new bodies we take on. You passed with honours."

"Pleased to hear it, new boss."

"New associate please."

"And last bit of business, promise. Tim's even sorted the contract offer for you. Here you go, have a look through these few pages when you fancy and run it past your accountant and lawyer of course, but I hope you like it."

"Brief headlines; similar to our consultants we have in legal, finance and PR, but you are worth more than them with what we do now and have coming up soon.

If you will, I'd like you to run presentation skills training for our senior team and come to main board meetings to advise on how we present the company. If you like us, think about joining our board as Nikos just has and we'll give you a share package.

I know you'll have speaking commitments too, and I'm sure that we can work round that, especially if you make sure you are billed as senior consultant for us on publicity material and the like.

With your package from us, you can just accept the offers you really fancy.

I might have to ring you a lot at odd times, but I'll love that anyway.

Full expense account of course, all air travel first class, and all hotels five star or above.

And, needs a drum roll here for the big finish. Initial five-year contract with guarantees, fifty grand sterling a month.

The boring stuff about pensions, health insurance and the rest is all in Tim's offer summary, but does that sound fair?"

"It sounds brilliant, pass the champagne."

"It sounds amazingly generous though; do you treat everybody this well?"

"Just the ones we don't want to lose. Seriously, we have a few people in your league and I honestly couldn't do without them. Tim is probably the highest paid executive assistant in the world, but I'd be lost without him.

Putting aside the way I feel for you personally, I want you with us, and me, for the long term. I like our top people to feel so well looked after that no competitor in the world could drag them away."

"Consider me permanent – loving it already."

"Great. The day is ours now – unless something big comes up, nobody will disturb me. Now tell me how you got into this weird business of yours."

"I think I picked up the comedy gene from my Uncle Bill.

Do you know, he could stand in the high street on a Saturday afternoon and bring the house down just by reading the telephone directory?"

"Really?"

"Yes, but then again he did have his cock out."

Barbara exploded into her shrieking giggle which he loved to hear.

"Brilliant – now tell me the real tale."

John told her the story from the night of the one-man band in the workies' club and his ascent of the ladder.

She laughed a lot, but felt a big chord being struck with her own rapid rise to the top of her business from the lowliest of starts.

"Tell me something which will surprise me about the speaking circuit. Goes without saying, we can be totally open with each other and not a word goes out of here. You give me a kind of peace which is new to me, and I know I can trust you. And I hope you know that you can trust me with anything."

"I knew that straight away; I really did. Right - let me tell you something odd."

"You know you were telling me that weird people hit on you late at night?

It happens to me – there's something about being a speaker which gets you into the rock god groupie status sometimes. And I'm not taking the piss at all."

"I get that completely" she said, "It's real turn-on for a woman to see a man dominate a room and take complete control. It does the trick for me. You do the trick for me."

"What's the strangest offer you've had?"

"I'll tell you a cracker. If it turns you on smile; if not, punch me. That's market research."

She giggled and leaned back with a glass of champagne expectantly.

"At the end of one speaking evening, a lady of about forty came across to chat. She was quite attractive, county set, well spoken, the lot.

She pointed to a very young lady at the end of top table; I'd noticed the two of them sitting together, really laughing in all the right places when I was doing my stint.

She was a stunner – great legs, pert breasts, short tight black skirt, glittery blue top, long hair in a pony-tail, super-model kind of poise. And when she crossed her legs there was definitely a flash of stockings and suspenders."

"You hardly noticed her then?'"

"Exactly."

Barbara and John dissolved into a joint giggling fit.

She came over to the sofa where he was looking very comfortable and sat next to him. She picked up a breadstick and pretended it was a microphone.

"And did sir feel like giving her one?"

They were now both in tears of laughter and holding each other for support.

"It gets better. Mrs County Set took about a minute to crack through her proposal.

It turned out that the girl was her daughter and had turned eighteen a few months back."

She said that there were a few potential boyfriends sniffing around – in her words - "all of them pure dorks and about as sophisticated as a pissed warthog."

"I don't know if this counts as an entry for the caring mother of the year award, but, word for word I promise, she said,

"Her fool of a father ran off with a slapper years ago and she's had no real example of a mature man.

I wonder if you'd care to take her to bed for me and give her a top-class seeing to? It would do her so much more good than a wham, bam fumble with one of those local idiots."

"She said it just like she was asking a jobbing gardener if he could trim the lawn and tidy up the hedge."

"Bloody hell" said Barbara, "My fault. I did ask you about the strangest offer you'd had."

"So, do I get a punch on the nose?"

"You don't. For future reference, this is my turned-on smile. My very turned-on smile."

"Did you take up the offer?"

"No, but she did raise the stakes and asked if I'd like to give her a good servicing too."

"You must have been tempted though."

"Yes, to be honest, but there's a kind of alarm bell rings in my head. I've seen so many big names in sport and show business who've scuppered the lot for the sake of a few minutes of pleasure."

I managed to get away, but, can't tell a lie, I imagined every moment during an extended J Arthur."

"A what?"

"Rhyming slang. J Arthur Rank."

She looked mystified for a moment, then shrieked with laughter as the penny dropped.

"I'm probably just paranoid, "said John, "but what if something like that is a set-up and you end up on video on social media or all over the papers?"

"Time was, back in the Sixties and Seventies or so, when anything went.

I was talking to a guy who worked comedy in holiday camps and the like and he was like a kid in a sweet shop. He was affectionately known as the slag-blaster – possibly slightly politically incorrect these days."

It was outrageous really. One so-called British rock god told me a classic. If I told you his name, I'd have to kill you.

He used to wear tight jeans and would put a huge continental sausage down his left leg to interest the girls in the audience.

One night, he's doing his act like a cut-price Elvis and there's a good-looking girl in the front row. She's wearing a mini-skirt and no knickers and, how can I put this, she's putting her wares on display and thrusting at rock god man on stage.

He's trying to perform, but can't take his eyes off the throbbing beaver in front of him.

He's so turned on that he grows a real stiffy down his right leg.

He's watching the girl with her jaw hanging open and bouncing her gaze from his left thigh to the right and back again.

She said something to her mate next to her.

Probably, "Look, Sharon, these rock stars have two dicks!"

The world really had changed over the last few decades and John told her his story of the Caribbean auction in London when rival city firms were bidding for thousand against each other to show who had the biggest swinging dick.

"Your guys in corporate governance but probably have a fit over something like that these days."

John told her of another classic example when he'd been speaking at a lunch in the City years back, before financial reality came along with an ugly day of reckoning.

It was a Friday and it was clear that nobody was going back to work at any point.

"I did my stint, great crowd, and the formal bit wound up about five.

The Chairman did his thanks speech and announced

that all present were welcome at the Banker's Draft pub next door."

"This was a huge place, a former bank, and it looked like a Greek temple."

Just about everyone from the lunch went across, about five hundred of them, and the Chairman had put a tab behind the bar.

This lot didn't bugger about; it wasn't a few pints; it was champagne and cognac, all the good stuff.

I was enjoying it, networking, sowing business cards and all the rest. Perhaps because I wasn't as ratted as the rest of them, but getting there, I noticed something odd."

The Chairman seemed a decent guy and I hate to see somebody being conned, so I sidled up to him and told him quietly,

"Not really my business, but there are now a couple of hundred people here who weren't at the lunch. They're just coming in off the street and phoning a friend by the look of it, and drinking on your tab like there's no tomorrow."

"I know" he said, "but it's not worth the hassle to check everyone. I'll probably be drinking on their tabs over the next few weeks."

They genuinely didn't care; they thought the money mine would cough up for ever.

"Back to your corporate governance though, Barbara, and I do meet some right head-bangers."

A bit back, I was compering a lovely function at Huddersfield Town Football Club. And stop it – jealousy is an ugly emotion.

Every tale that John remembered was drawing smiles and twinkling eyes from Barbara and they were both loving it – a lot.

I went in the afternoon to do the usual run-through and sound check. The cabaret was The Bachelors who'd had monster hits a bit back and they were great. They were a trio but one of them had dropped out.

I know – an Irish trio with only two members. Anyway, the function room was an odd shape; very long and low with a ceiling which wasn't too high either.

Their sound guy was as real pro and he'd set up about a dozen speakers along the wide wall behind top table. It meant that the sound was nicely spread instead of the daft set-up you sometimes see where there are two monster speakers which deafen the people near them, and nobody else can hear a thing.

He was all set up and had a brilliant piece of kit to check that all of the speakers were putting sound out.

He ran a test and made it sound like a jet aircraft was coming in one end of the room and going out the other.

I asked him to have it ready for the start of the evening as I had a cunning plan.

It was a celebration night because the team had just been promoted and the room was full of the team's colours – blue and white streamers and balloons everywhere.

For the routine I had in mind, I was dead lucky because it was tanking down outside. I warmed the audience up and it really was a great atmosphere.

"A spot of sad news." I said, "We had hoped to take you all out on to the pitch and we had booked the Red

Arrows to fly over the ground trailing blue and white smoke in celebration.

You've all seen the weather, and the health and safety people have done a risk assessment and ruled that the weather is too bad for it to go ahead in rainy skies.

There was a sigh of disappointment at my special announcement, which was a load of bollocks by the way.

"However, there is good news."

A big cheer came from the audience who would have applauded anything that night. "We have clearance for the Red Arrows to perform their display indoors!"

Another big cheer.

On the cue of "indoors", I'd fixed for the stadium staff to open the enormous doors at the short ends of the function room. They really were huge doors, designed to allow vehicles to enter for car shows and the like."

"Just one request please, to ensure the safety of our brave pilots. As you know, this room has a low ceiling, so would you please put your head on your table and pull the balloons down to face level.

This will ensure full safety compliance."

It looked brilliant. Every head in the room was flat on a table and the balloons were well and truly tugged down.

"Ladies and gentlemen, for the first time in Huddersfield, the Red Arrows!"

As planned, the clever sound guy racked up the volume and it really did sound like a crop of jet planes had screamed through the room.

The bass on the sound kit was out of this world; every plate and glass rattled and the sound waves even popped a few balloons.

Bloody brilliant, appreciated by roaring laughter and a massive round of applause.

What a great start to the night and I was chuffed to bits that the idea had worked like a dream.

We were just settling down for the soup when this woman with a face like a smacked arse marched over to me.

"That was grossly irresponsible and sheer stupidity to fly jet aircraft through a room full of people."

I laughed; she didn't.

A few days later, there were formal complaints to the football club, the local council, and me.

"I love that," said Barbara, "you can ride over a crackpot like that, but does anything ever get you down?"

"Do you know?" said John, a few years back I was genuinely upset and I still can't get it out of my head.

I was speaking at a travel trade conference in Weimar, in the old East Germany in communist days.

The place had an even darker history going back to the Thirties and Forties.

I stayed in the Hotel Elephant and there was a balcony where Hitler had given one of his rabble-rousing speeches during the rise of the Nazi Party.

They don't have postcards of that on the rack in reception.

Anyway, the dinner itself was at a beautiful old castle just up the hill from the town.

What I discovered was that, during the war, this place was a base for the Nazi officers who were murdering people in their thousands just along the road at Buchenwald Concentration Camp.

I still can't get my head round that. How can cultured people routinely exterminate innocent people and then go off to a lovely castle and eat dinner and drink wine?"

"That's awful, it really is. Tell me a happy story, then we can go down for dinner."

John had genuinely not noticed that they'd been laughing and enjoying each other's company for hours now.

"You're right, the music hall guys always said leave 'em laughing."

John told her about the best practical joke he'd seen, and he'd seen a few.

"I was speaking at Castle Combe, not far from Chippenham. It's a popular venue for car companies because there's a huge circuit where dealers and journalists can try out their new models. It's private land, of course, so there are no speed restrictions.

The event was for Mercedes and Chrysler. They had their top contacts having a great afternoon with their new top end models hurtling round the track. In the evening, there was a lovely dinner and I did my turn.

It was just a few weeks before Christmas and, when I went back to my room, they'd left a gorgeous top-end hamper as a gift.

It really was the best – Harrod's if I remember rightly.

The next morning, after breakfast, people were saying their goodbyes and exchanging Christmas greetings in the reception area.

Most of them were old hands but one guy, Jerry, was new to all this.

He was walking through reception just about managing his case and hamper together.

"Have you enjoyed it then, Jerry?" asked Tony Masterson, an old hand at these jollies and a guy with a wicked sense of fun.

"It's been brilliant, a cracking couple of days."

"Are you putting those in your car and then coming back for your other gift?" asked Tony, deadpan.

"Which other gift's that."

"Well, the hamper is courtesy of Mercedes, but didn't you see the flat-screen television from Chrysler? It should have been on the desk in your room.

No problem, though, just leave it if you don't want it."

Young Jerry walked briskly to his car, put his case and the hamper in his boot, and was back into the hotel and up the stairs at some speed.

He was walking back through reception carrying the expensive television with about ten pairs of eyes watching him.

One pair of eyes belonged to the hotel security man.

"Do you have a minute sir?"

Bastards.

Barbara and John didn't go down for dinner but had supper sent up to the suite.

They eventually fell asleep in each other's arms.

John woke in the early hours and lifted Barbara onto the bed, covering her with a blanket.

She had a smile on her face and was sleeping like a

baby; content, very happy and still chaste.

He left her a note;

Ring me as soon as you wake up – don't want to waste a minute tomorrow – sweet dreams. Xx

He leaned over her and kissed her cheek, lingering so that he could taste her skin. He wondered if she tasted that good everywhere.

He didn't know it yet, but he would find out tomorrow.

John tip-toed out, went back to his room and slept, eventually.

CHAPTER 16 – FLYING APART

When John returned to his room, there was a folder from Tim waiting on his desk. Did that man ever sleep?

He scanned through it and it was confirmation of everything Barbara had promised, including a crop of perks which he hadn't even thought of, including memberships of a top gym chain as well as private clubs in London and other major cities around the world.

He slept on and off; trying to compose in his head a tidy summary of what had happened in such a short time.

Home seemed a long way off, even though he'd be back there by tonight.

He'd put his phone back on to charge, along with a new company mobile which was part of his welcome package.

He'd forgotten to turn off his personal phone, which is why his half sleep was interrupted by a ping which showed that a text had landed.

Probably junk at seven in the morning, but he looked anyway.

It was from his bank and was part of a system which alerted him if any unusual activity had taken place.

It certainly had, in the form of a deposit of £600,000 into his account.

He looked at it and didn't dare put his phone down in case the money disappeared.

He switched on his laptop and logged in to his account to get more detail.

Happily, it appeared there too, showing the

depositor's name as MCP Global, Barbara's company.

On the welcome pack left by Tim was his business card complete with personal mobile number and a hand-written note;

Hope all makes sense John. Welcome aboard and very much look forward to working together. Any queries, do ring me. I'm awake funny hours but, if I'm having a nap, leave a message and I'll get back to you soonest. Best – Tim.

John rang the number expecting his call to go to voicemail, but Tim answered.

"Good morning John, how are you this beautiful morning," sounding very sharp for this time of day.

"Excellent thanks Tim, and thanks so much for your very comprehensive welcome pack. Just one little query just to make sure that your finance guys haven't made a mistake."

"It's rare that they do John but I can check for you, no trouble."

"It's just that my contract is for £50k a month, paid on the last day of each month, but £600k has landed in my account this morning. Have they paid a year in advance by mistake?"

"No John. It's probably buried in the terms and conditions in your pack, but it's your welcome bonus equal to a year's salary. Monthly pay will start popping in at the end of the current month.

No rush, but our finance guys will be in touch with your accountant and legal guys to sort out the best payment route.

That bonus is tax paid. They'll find the best way to minimise tax exposure on future payments and keep it all clean and legal."

Have a good day and look forward to seeing you in London next Friday."

"You have a great day too Tim and thanks for all your help. Look forward to working together."

As well as trying to take in the fact that a lovely woman he had never met until a few days ago was now in his life, he was coming to terms with over half a million landing in his account out of the blue. Not to mention being in London next Friday, which was news to him.

There was not much chance of sleeping now, and he read the English papers online and filled in his time until about ten. He was just about to take a coffee onto his terrace when the phone pinged again, this time from Barbara.

Just popping into town for a few things. My place at eleven? Xx"

Quick reply – *yes please, see you soon gorgeous. Xx*

Trying hard to switch his head back to England, he phoned home, knowing it was early with the time difference.

"Hi – you get the text ok? Should be back about 10 tonight if the plane's on time."

"Looks like it's gone really well there with them keeping you longer and with that consultancy contract you emailed."

"It's been amazing. They've just left me a hard copy of the contract and it's even better than the summary sounds."

"They're not too hot on accuracy though. I presume

it's for five grand a month, but there's an extra zero – the summary says fifty."

"I hope you're sitting down. The fifty is correct and, better yet, and sit down harder, six hundred grand tax-free landed in the account this morning – it's my signing-on bonus.

Looks like I might need to be in London for them end of next week. I'll know more later, but at that fee level, I'll be where they want me."

"It's all happened quickly hasn't it?"

"Well, yes and no; they've been keeping tabs on me for quite a while apparently, and these last few days have been the final beauty parade.

I've had Brian the accountant back to me already and he says it's a watertight contract. It's all new to me at this level but he says it's a five-year guarantee, renewable by mutual consent.

It means that, in the unlikely event of them ending it tomorrow, I'd be entitled to a minimum three million for the five years, plus all benefits for that period."

"Bloody hell."

"I know; I'm still taking it in. They'll want some work for their money, but I'm confident I can do it, and so are they."

"What's your new boss like?"

"She won't let me call her my boss; we are associates I'm told."

"She? What's she like?"

"Her name's Barbara and she's phenomenal; started with nowt and built up the business to where it is now. Doing the sums, she must be a billionaire plus."

John decided to move the conversation on before he blushed out loud. "Much happening at home?"

"Just the usual, except I bumped into Terry in Tesco and he sends his best. You must be about the same age, aren't you?"

"Well, yes, we were at school together and I've known him all this time. Why you ask?"

"He looks awful and about ten years older than you. It's all over the grapevine that Susie has moved out and gone to live with her mother. She's a conniving old cow that mother of hers and she's probably doing more to keep them apart than get them back together.

He asked when you were due back and would you fancy a pint to cheer him up?"

"I'll give him a ring and suggest mid-week. Don't think cheering him up is likely, but he is an old mate."

"Well, I'll let you get busy. Give me a ring when you land at Newcastle and I'll put the kettle on."

The routine conversation had made John feel odd; same old, same old at home, but here in Corfu it felt like a different world.

The whole day felt distinctly weird and it was about to get weirder.

It was almost eleven and time to see Barbara.

Leaving his room, he felt like Clark Kent stepping out of a phone box and assuming a new identity as Superman.

Barbara greeted him with a kiss as if he'd they not been together for weeks.

"All well my new associate?"

"Wonderfully so here and all seems to be fine at

home....... "

Barbara put her finger to her lips; "Shush, don't want to know yet. We'll cross that bridge another time."

John was almost lost for words, unusually for him, and changed the subject.

"Forgot to ask, why is your company called MCP – is it meant to stand for Male Chauvinist Pig?"

Her giggle was back, which sounded good.

It was originally going to be the initials of Manchester Petro Chemicals, but MPC was already taken at Companies' House, so we just changed two initials round.

I wanted to keep M for Manchester in there to respect our roots, and Chemicals Petro sounds more intriguing somehow. And the Americans presume that the Manchester is Manchester, New Hampshire, as they would.

It did occur to me that Male Chauvinist Pig Global summed up quite a few men I've come up against over the years – but I wiped them all out eventually.

I tell my mum it stands for Mum's Colossal Pension and she's happy with that."

"Did you get your shopping you wanted in town?"

"I did" and there was that smile on full power again, "it was for you really."

"Enjoy your coffee and listen to this – back in a moment."

She flicked a button on the music system which started the unmistakable introduction to Dylan's *Lay Lady Lay* and slipped into the suite's bedroom.

Lay lady lay

Lay across my big brass bed

Dylan's softer voice showing that he could do seductive as well as everything else in his armoury.

She came back into the room showing off her great legs and pert breasts, wearing a tight short black skirt, and a glittery blue top. She had her long blonde hair in a ponytail and walked slowly with super model poise.

She slid her skirt up slightly and, with that giggle again, revealed stockings and suspenders.

"Remind you of anything?"

She held out her hand and he took it as she led him into her bedroom.

There was indeed a big brass bed. Surely, she'd not had it brought in specially? Who knew with this wonder woman?

She sat on the bed and pulled him next to her. She looked him straight in the eyes and deep inside his head.

"Listen you; enough people have tried and failed, but I've never felt so erotically charged in my life. I'm thinking about you all the time and can't get your story of the young girl and her mother's offer out of my head.

Tonight, we'll be a few thousand miles apart; you'll be back home and I have to be in Dubai for two days to put that deal to bed.

You opened up to me and told me about turning down the offer for all the right reasons, then making yourself come just thinking about it.

Me too.

Being a bit direct, I've brought myself to orgasm three times during the night putting myself into your fantasy.

Please enjoy the moment, make love to me, and I can

glow with it tonight and feel you still inside me.

We are in the safest place possible; enjoy your young submissive girl and talk to me.

This is our world and there's just us here – except for perhaps that girl and her mother.

She giggled and then he kissed her hard.

She took his hand and gently placed it between her legs.

They talked during sex and, afterwards, kept talking and stayed wide awake.

"Please let it always be that good" breathed Barbara, with a tear of happiness rolling down her cheek.

"You must have been right about meeting in a former life. How can I be that close to a woman after a few days? It's not possible."

"It is" said Barbara, "and I'm just grateful as hell that we found each other. Don't let anything spoil this."

She rolled sideways and looked at the clock.

"Again please, before it's airport time."

Time moved on despite them and, by three, they had to prepare to leave for their flights.

A car had been booked to take them on the short run for their flights from Corfu; John to Newcastle and Barbara to Athens for a connection to Dubai.

"Call me later when you can. Use your company phone 'cos it's a secure line. When you ring me, it's so tight you wouldn't believe it – no secret service in the world could crack it.

When I can't have you holding me, we can talk like we did today and it'll be the next best thing. I'm looking forward to that – a lot."

"You can come to London end of next week can't you."

"Yes, Tim mentioned it, no problem."

"Just give Tim a ring later – he'll sort everything you need through our transport guy from now on. Come down plane or train on Thursday and there will be a car to pick you up.

We have a company apartment next to mine in the City and you can stay there."

"Some of the time" she giggled.

We can have dinner on Thursday, then come to your first main board meeting on Friday.

On Saturday evening, we have a table at a big industry awards do at the Park Lane Hilton. We are in for an award, and I should think so too.

That place will bring some great memories back for you.

Then a lazy-ish day on Sunday and we can go from there."

"I want to make life so good for you John."

"If we had a bedsit and a bike, you'd be doing that."

"I know and I love you for it."

"Love you too; talk to you soon and see you on Thursday."

In his comfortable seat on the Newcastle bound flight, John smiled as he replayed in his mind every moment of the day, including the "love you" to each other with no drama, just inevitability.

As the plane began its descent after the short flight, he pondered changing back into his Clark Kent suit and wondered if he could park Superman for a while.

CHAPTER 17 – HOME RUN

Even the short trip from Newcastle Airport to home had entered a new league.

In his pre-MCP life, all those days ago, he had to book his own taxi – what hardship.

Before he'd left Corfu, he'd had another pleasant company text;

Greetings John. Sally here from Tim's empire. 😊

I'll be your personal PA for travel arrangements and the like. My direct mobile and email below – contact me for anything you need. I've booked your car to pick you up at Newcastle tonight. There'll be a chap with the MCP logo board as you leave security.

When you are ready, let me know how you want to travel to London next Thursday and I'll sort it. I'll be helping at next Friday's meeting, so look forward to saying hello. Sleep well. Sally.

The "chap with the car" turned out to be a uniformed chauffeur with a top of the range Mercedes.

"Welcome home, sir. I'm Chris and I'll most likely be doing a lot of your local runs. Here's my card with the direct number just in case there are any late changes or whatever."

As they neared John's home, he was tempted to ask Chris to blast the horn a few times to alert the neighbours to his new mode of transport, but he thought better of it.

He did text Janet, though, to give her an exact time of arrival and she was at the front door to meet him. She clocked the car and let out a quiet "wow" in appreciation, before bowing with a smile.

"Welcome home sir."

Despite his long and remarkable day, he stayed wide awake to have a nightcap with Janet and talked through the dream job.

"I got hold of Terry, by the way, and he does sound thoroughly fed up with life. I said I've have a quick pint with him tomorrow evening. I'll need to be up and about on Thursday to go to London for a few days."

"It's even worse for the poor lad though. As well as Susie moving out, it looks like his work is going down the tubes too.

I'll play down the new consultancy with MCP by the way; I'd feel awful crowing about that with him in the pits. If anybody asks you, you can mention MCP and what I'm doing, but leave the figures just for us to know."

"Why, aren't you dying to flaunt it?"

"I'd love to, but you know how some people are. Not everybody likes others to do well.

I remember a great story about Tom Jones and what happened when he went back to his home village when he was at the top of tree and making a mint.

He said that, if he bought everyone in the pub a drink, he was a flash git, and, if he didn't, he was a tight git."

John was feeling a strange split in his head. Home felt just as it was when he set off for Corfu just days before, but half of him was there or in Dubai with Barbara.

He'd have to work that one through, but, for now, he felt like an actor who had made the slick transition from one role to another.

This wasn't a piece of theatre, though, it was real life.

It felt even more of back to the normal, when, at Terry's request, they met for their catch-up in the Shipbuilder's Arms the next evening.

John had managed to speak to Barbara on the phone earlier in the day and her lyrical description of the sunshine and her beautiful hotel room was a long way from here.

"Good to see you John, "said Terry. "You must be knackered; Janet said you'd had a few days running around in Corfu and you are down in London again on Thursday."

"I can't complain. When I think of my dad working hard in a shipyard, he'd laugh if I described what I do as hard work."

"I've just taken on something new; a consultancy for a big outfit called MCP and I have a lot to learn, but it's fascinating."

"Does the Shipbuilder's feel like a dump to you now after all your running around in the glamour spots?"

"No; I still enjoy coming back. Everybody says it, but your home patch keeps you grounded and stops any chance of becoming big headed. I really enjoy our chats and joint memories, I really do. And I get much more comedy material in this pub than I do in the deep south!"

"The funny thing is that some of your comedy lines come back round again John.

That one you do about the first thing you see when you get back to Hartlepool Railway Station has spread like wildfire."

It was one of John's favourites when he announced that he always knew when he was back home when he saw the white van outside the station with the message on its side, "No pies are kept in this van overnight."

"And what was that one you do about the croissant? I don't have the memory that you do – it must be like a bloody filing cabinet inside your head."

It was John's routine about the fact that the posh croissant was simply an empty pastie. He had even built up a story about a plot developed by crafty southerners.

They would come to the north, buy a pastie for well under a pound, eat the filling, and take the now empty pastry cases back home to sell as croissants at three pounds a time.

"So, what's this new job with the big outfit; what do they do?

"Well, they're in petrochemicals all over the world. They started in Manchester, and the boss is an amazing woman who started as a dogsbody with them and now runs the company – as well as owning most of it."

"But you know bugger all about petrochemicals."

Back home, they always told it like it is.

"I know, but I do know about presentation and that's what they need. They'd been tracking me for a while by the sound of it, and made the offer during the Corfu trip."

The main job is to train their top guys in presentation skills and sit in on board meetings to advise on getting the company image right."

Even the word "offer" had him drifting into memories of fantasy sessions with Barbara; Terry presumed that the big smile was just about the new job.

John thought it was time to turn the focus around to

Terry; he really didn't want to blow his own trumpet when he knew that life had not been so good for his old mate.

Even so, he couldn't help but think how far they had moved along different paths since that broom cupboard in the workies' club all those years ago.

"I'm sorry to hear about Susie; Janet tells me that she's upped sticks and moved in with her mum."

"Yeah, that frigging cow bag, the evil bastard."

"You're not keen on her then."

"I've really tried over the years, but she always thought I wasn't good enough for her lovely daughter. She thought a jobbing musician was always way below all the lovely men she could have married."

"I always thought you and Susie were set for life; you seemed to tick along just fine."

"Perhaps that's just it John. We just ticked along as you say; no excitement, just routine, and no sex for a bloody long time either. Perhaps we just have to accept that sex stops for people our age."

John took a sip of his pint to avoid grinning.

"If you only knew," he thought.

"Tell me to shut up if it's not my business, but it is there someone else involved?"

"We've known each other long enough to talk straight John. Nobody else in my life, and I'm just about certain not for her."

"Do you want her back?"

"That's the daft thing; I don't really know. Perhaps it has just run its course and we might both make fresh starts. There are no kids to worry about and house is paid for. We could sell up, tidy things up, and see where we go next.

It's hard to say it out loud, but how many of our friends are still married? It's not like it used to be when people just stayed married regardless. Divorce is all around us."

"Might me another one soon" wondered John.

"What's keeping you busy these days Terry" asked John, pretending to know nowt.

"That's another thing. The glory days of those workies' club have about gone. You never got rich doing that, but it was regular cash. And the private pupils have really dwindled; perhaps kids would rather play with their phones than musical instruments now."

"We pay the bills and just about get by for cash. Even though she never says so, I wonder if Susie looks at other people with swish cars and regular holidays and feels let down."

"Well, if you are really looking for a new start, have you thought about cruise ships? I've told you before that they are crying out for people like you.

You can play a couple of instruments really well, you can read music, and you've done musical director type jobs, haven't you?"

"I'll probably be opting out of most of my cruise speaking stuff soon with my new stuff keeping me busy, but I know lots of cruise directors and booking agents well. With me singing your praises, you could be on a nice ship in no time.

Get paid, see the world, meet lots of people, perhaps even end up with Mrs Terry the Second?"

He laughed at that thought.

"You make it sound so bloody easy John."

"Perhaps because it could be?"

"I know. But I like my routine. Coming in here to see the lads, lots of familiar places around me."

"It's up to you Terry. I'm not trying to tell you what to do; just saying that there are options out there. I never dreamt that I'd be doing what I'm doing now all those years ago when we were waiting for the strippers to finish their acts before I made my comedy debut.

And that was all down to you. I'll never forget that."

"I'm loving life now." And then some, thought John.

"Look, I'll have to make a move shortly. I need to be up in the morning to sort a few things for the new job.

If you change your mind about cruise ships, give me a shout. Why not try one cruise and see if it suits you? Either way, keep in touch and ring anytime. Old friends don't want to lose touch."

John shook Terry's hand and hugged him.

"I'm on your side remember."

He left Terry to join a table of pals and headed off home, ready to resume his new life in London the next day.

CHAPTER 18 – LONDON PRIDE

On the Thursday morning, John was up early with London, and Barbara, on his mind.

It still felt odd, this dual life business, and it unsettled him because it didn't seem to unsettle him.

He took tea up to Janet in bed and sat chatting a while – again on dual track – partly about the follow up after his chat with Terry a couple of nights before, and looking ahead to what the new role with MCP would involve.

His cruise speaker agent Maria had phoned the day before about some potential dates and John had asked to hang fire for a while.

He told her, kind of truthfully, that he had a new commitment which would take a lot of time, and he'd see how diary was looking before committing himself.

While she was on, he asked if they were still looking for musicians and musical directors.

"I have a friend who may well be keen, and he's likely to have a lot of free time soon. He's a really good instrumentalist and he'd be a top notch musical director too."

"They'd bite his hand off," said Maria. "I have a crop of cruise lines looking for people, so ask him to ring me and mention your name. If you rate him, that's good enough for me."

John told Janet the story and said that he'd phoned Terry straight away.

"After our session in the pub, I thought it would be perfect for him. He needs some work, and I have an awful feeling that the split with Susie will be permanent.

It would do him good to get away, have some thinking time, and see that there's another world out there. The least he could do is to give it a go."

"So, is he going to ring your cruise lady and get the first one in the diary?"

"Doesn't look like it. He was on about missing the company of his mates in the Shipbuilder's if he went away for long spells. I wouldn't mind, but they're the most miserable pack of gits.

I've tried to chat with them to be sociable with Terry, but they'd have the happiest bloke in the world set to top himself.

It's like a game where you try to out-misery the bloke next to you and have a kind of bidding session about who has the most to be fed up about.

You've been on enough cruise ships to know it could be the making of him. Most of the people he'd be working with are good company, and he'd even have a new set of passengers to talk to every week or two. Then again, perhaps it's the thought of meeting new people which is putting him off."

"Don't fret about it John, you can't tell people how to live their lives."

"I know. I'm not trying to be a control freak, but he's going to be old before his time if that's going to be his total social life in misery corner in the pub."

"Leave him to it. You've bent over backwards to give him a great option. Anyway, how about your next few days. What are you going to be doing?"

John's compartments in his head were in action again. He'd better keep off what he hoped to be doing some of the time.

"Well, there's a planning dinner tonight, then my first board meeting tomorrow. Tim has sent me the agenda and the minutes of the last few meetings to give me a flavour.

Then there's an awards dinner in Park Lane on Saturday night. That will be an odd experience – no work to do. Just enjoy the networking and we are up for an award."

It occurred to him that he was now saying "we" – in only a few days, he had come to feel part of the MCP family."

"Don't take this the wrong way John, but what can you add to a multi-national monster of a petrochemical company? It's totally outside your experience."

"I know, but that's part of the point. What I do is totally outside *their* experience. You wouldn't believe how much homework they've put in. They have more videos of me with a microphone in my hand than I do.

There are other things as well as getting their presentation better. From a few things I've seen in board minutes, I think I can save them more than they are paying me."

"Bloody hell, you'll be due another bonus. When do you think you'll be back home?"

"Might be Monday but can't be sure. They've asked me to always have my passport with me just in case something urgent comes up. This new set up in Dubai is really taking off; can you believe I might have to go there for a few days soon?"

"Just as well it's not Terry they're taking on; he'd probably tell them he couldn't do Dubai because he'd miss darts night in the Shipbuilder's."

"Spot on. What's on your agenda while I'm away?"

"Feet up, three coffee mornings, and I have some shopping in mind with that bonus in the bank."

"You go for it – we had enough tight times early on when you had to count every penny you spent. Get stuck in and enjoy it."

"Is that flight case enough for a few days; especially if you are away longer?"

"I forget to tell you about another splendid perk. This company apartment they have in London has a room for me and they have accounts with top end tailors, shirt-makers, you name it.

Tim says that the most efficient thing to do is to keep a full wardrobe down there so that I'm ready for anything. They'll organise business suits, dinner suits, you name it. They even have an account with a laundry – in Knightsbridge, where else."

"You'd better get some lightweight suits for Dubai as well. The problems of a jet-setter!" she grinned.

"They're sorting a company apartment in Dubai so I can get fixed up there. Did I just say that? I'm getting used to all this."

"The funniest thing is that I get while all this makes sense now. Tim's philosophy is right – it is about efficient use of time rather than luxury for the sake of it.

If you are paying someone top whack, why would you want him spending time on booking travel or doing other routine things in life?

Someone on a fair bit less than top whack can do all those things and leave your top talent to get on with what you pay them for."

"So, you are top talent now?"

"Well spotted" he grinned, but it was true.

"Chris the driver will be here soon to take me to Darlington station, so I'll do a last check that I have everything I need. Talk to you soon, and enjoy your mega-shop."

He pecked her on the cheek and headed downstairs and down south.

He'd decided on the train because, for meetings in central London, he'd always found it was quicker than the plane. It might be only an hour in the air, but, by the time you added on getting through security and the waiting time, the train journey of under three hours was actually shorter."

The last time he'd done this trip, he'd booked his own ticket and hotel, and fixed a local taxi to Darlington.

PA Sally had sorted the lot.

The train ticket had been sent to his phone and a car would be picking him up at King's Cross for the short hop to the company apartment near Chancery Lane in the increasingly trendy mid-town, handy for the City and just about everything else.

The other thing about the train was that it was a good place to work. First class, of course, had room for his computer and everything else he needed, and there was a steady stream of coffee to his seat. Long-haul business class made a good travelling office, but domestic flights were just too cramped.

The staff on Virgin East Coast knew him well and, often Geordie, they had an ideal combination of customer service and warmth.

It worked both ways though; John remembered many

of their names and always asked about their day and, for the ones he knew best, how the family were doing.

They noticed the difference between the decent people like John who respected them, and the other kind who rarely grunted their thanks, never mind spoke to them. It is nice to be nice.

At the station he phoned Barbara and asked what she was doing.

"Two meetings to do and, as I'm chairing them, they'll finish on time. I'll be waiting at the apartment for you, dressed appropriately as sir desires. Would you like the mother or the daughter waiting for you?"

"Surprise me."

He could hear her smile from two hundred and fifty miles away. And she could feel his.

On the way down, he managed to concentrate and went through the board papers again. making notes on where he could see scope for big improvements.

He knew he was on show and a bit on trial, and he was determined to show the rest of the board that Barbara's confidence in him was well placed.

He wondered if her mind was running on double track during her meetings. Keeping her head sharp while feeling her thighs tingle.

He had clearly got the second part right. When she opened her apartment door, she held a finger to her lips.

"Before a word of work, come and service me and tell me how much my daughter enjoyed it while you are doing it."

Someone once said that the biggest sexual organ in the body is the brain, and they proved it for over an hour.

After a rainfall shower and with coffee in front of them, they smiled and said not a lot for some minutes.

"You are glowing young lady."

"I'm not surprised, and so are you by the way."

"Your tan suits you. You had a bit of time off in Dubai then?"

"Just a bit, but the business side is looking great. And, my best surprise, they know you from being a speaker there and were genuinely impressed that we had you on board.

In the words of a member of the royal family, you are a fine man and we have done well to capture you."

"Salam alaykum."

"They mentioned that - as well as everything else, you have taken the trouble to learn some Arabic and understand their culture."

"Just seems an obvious bit of courtesy, but not to all westerners they meet."

John had impressed them with his taste for lovely strong Arabic coffee – without sugar either. Hell, the caffeine in that stuff is amazing; after a couple, you run up to people you don't know and ask them if they want anything doing – quickly.

"I presume that anybody from MCP representing us there will have a familiarisation course before they go?"

Barbara smiled. "Love the way you talk about *us* as part of it all so quickly."

"I know – I've noticed that as well."

"And I'd love you to lead that fam course too."

"Be delighted to do that. One of the best ways to teach

people is to give them a few examples of how some people make a total balls-up of it, and I've seen a few."

Barbara snuggled in to his chest and listened as John told her about his own learning curve in the Middle East.

It included not referring to the region as the Middle East for a start. It comes over as a condescending throwback to colonial days.

"Just imagine if power had emerged in the opposite direction – Europe would just love being called the Middle West, and our American cousins would be chuffed to bits to be called the Far West!

Some guys from the States can be bad beyond belief at respecting other cultures. I nearly threw a brick through my own television watching an American film.

It was set in the UAE and this American big cheese was going ballistic because his opposite numbers there didn't speak perfect English.

Neither did he by the sound of it, but learning some Arabic would have been a basic courtesy."

"I've been going there on the speaking circuit for about twenty-five years. When I first went out, there was the Airport Hotel and the big Hyatt near the Creek with the revolving rooftop restaurant and that was about it.

And Jumeirah was just a fishing village – look at it now, it's a city.

The last time I was there, I chaired a conference for UAE government and they put me up in the Burj al Arab for six days. You've been there haven't you? Amazing, isn't it? Seven stars and what's that slogan they have? If it looks like gold, it is."

"Funny though, the worst ever case I saw of getting in wrong was by a Brit not an American.

I've done a crop of events for a big investment company in Sharjah – they'll be a good contact for us by the way – and you'll know it's a bit different to Dubai.

It's more traditional and reserved, partly because there's a lot of Saudi investment there, but they are very adaptable too.

For us Brits, men especially, you have pick up a few signals and take it steadily, especially with women you meet in business.

You'll know this, but not everyone gets that some women are quite westernised, but many have very traditional values and, of course, you respect that.

People should know that, if a woman is of traditional culture, she will only have physical contact with a man if it's her husband or a family member.

It's straightforward once you've been taught. If you are introduced to a woman, keep your hands by your sides and nod a greeting. If she holds out her hand to shake yours the western way, that's fine; if she doesn't, leave your hands where they are and don't think of making physical contact.

One day when I'm in their office, this Brit character turns up who's acting like a cross between Del Boy and a Harry Enfield character.

The chairman of this company is a lovely guy – a real presence about him, which you'd expect as he's also a member of the royal family.

I've had planning meetings with him in London – he has a lovely place in Regent's Park and is always immaculate in a well-cut business suit.

In Sharjah, he's wearing traditional Arab robes of course, and running meetings the local way.

You'll have seen these guys in action; breezing through an office the size of a football pitch and stopping by a small group of people, taking in information and making decisions at speed.

And always, of course, the guy at his shoulder with the silver tray holding a beautiful coffee pot and the tiny cups.

Must remember to teach our people the coffee etiquette too. Always take one even if you don't like coffee – it's an insult to your host's hospitality if you don't, and hold your cup out for a couple of refills to show that you think it's delicious.

On the fourth offer, wiggle your cup from side to side to decline any more.

Anyway, the Del Boy character is introduced to the Sheikh, who introduces him to Fatima, his finance director, who happens to be of very traditional stock.

Del not only puts his arm around her shoulder, but kisses her on the cheek and says, "How you're doin' sweetheart?"

He might as well have really gone for it and juggled her breasts."

Barbara nearly spilled her coffee as she laughed at the picture he'd painted.

"Brilliant. You should write a book called something like *Learning by Laughing*."

"Let's strike while the iron's hot" said Barbara. "The two of us could go out for a few days next week. You can get to know our new company guys in Dubai and set up lunch with your investment people in Sharjah.

I'll get Tim to book us into the Burj while we do some apartment hunting."

"Sound good?"

"Sounds brilliant."

"While we are in business mode, can I run some ideas past you before I say anything at the board meeting tomorrow?"

"Please do"

"I'd planned to listen and not say too much at my first meeting, but, having read through those past minutes, some things jump out at me."

It was Barbara who did the listening and nodded her agreement.

"That's a great menu of ideas. Why didn't we think of that lot before? Yes, please wheel them out tomorrow; they'll go down a storm."

"That's the point of a board of different talents, isn't it?

There'll be people there with expertise I don't have, in petrochemicals for one, but when it comes to presentation and reputational management I can really help.

I've had years of seeing what works and what doesn't at close quarters.

I've had some great tuition too. I've lost count of the number of government ministers and big business names I've sat next to over the years. I'd ask few questions at a dinner and get a couple of hours of free guidance."

"Gets better every day. Let's have dinner and you'll be all set to wow them tomorrow."

CHAPTER 19 - BOARD AND BED

"Let's go wild," said Barbara, "there's a great restaurant just five minutes' walk from here. The fresh air will do us good and I can show you off."

Her lovely giggle would always have him fully in agreement with any idea she had.

She was right; the place was special and the welcome given to Barbara showed that she was clearly a regular.

She introduced him to the maitre d' as "my very good friend John.".

Two complimentary cool glasses of champagne were soon in their hands, and they raised a toast to each other.

"Do I detect a sad look in those lovely eyes, young lady?"

"Just a bit. I know I'm being greedy, but I'd love the day to come when I can introduce you as something more than my good friend.

"My man" would be good, and "my husband" would be a dream."

John tried to speak but she held a finger to his lips.

"I'm honestly not trying to push. You are a good man, and I know you wouldn't want to hurt Janet if you could help it."

It was the first time she'd mentioned her, let alone used her name, and it rattled them both. John's parallel worlds were being pulled together.

"I just want you to be a full and public part of my life John.

I'm trying not to be selfish, but I want all of you. If it

can be done, I wouldn't want to hurt anybody either — she could have a life she wanted, we could sort that."

Barbara hadn't repeated the pain by using her name a second time.

"I want to be able to show you off, to walk into big rooms on your arm, to be introduced as a real couple.

I'm sure that Tim and Sally know how things are; they fix all our travel and most things else.

They are both far too professional to say anything, but I want everyone to know, and to see how happy I am.

I've had a few false start relationships over the years, but never anything strong or looking permanent. I've never felt as sure of anything in my life as I do about you.

Someone said that the perfect relationship happens once. For both of us, I know with certainty that this is our *once*."

John wasn't expecting this, but he should have been.

"I know exactly how you are thinking. It's on my mind all the time. You are right, I don't like to hurt anyone and I've been told before that I need a harder edge.

In some ways, it would be simple. No children to think about, and, especially now, I'm sure I'd never need to let her down financially and make life hard for her."

"I've thought already that I frighten myself; being able to act normally at home and know I'm gasping to see you.

It is an act though and I don't know how long I can keep it up without pouring it all out to her."

"Do you remember, John, I told you that I always have a Plan B?

With you, I don't. If I can't have you, I don't want anybody else.

Bollocks, that's nearly another song title, isn't it?"

Her smile broke the tension, but they both knew that they had gone a long way up the mountain in the last few minutes.

"Whatever happens, John, I don't want to lose what we have.

Forgive me if I'm sounding dramatic but I just don't know what I'd do without you now."

"I'm just the same Barbara. We know where we want to be don't we? It will happen."

"That's all I need to know. I'm glad I let it out. Let's enjoy where we are and get it right for everybody. That ok?"

It was, and the burst of real life through into their private world felt good. It wasn't going to be easy, but no good things ever were."

The restaurant was busy, but they had no idea who else was there; their own world was precious and they enjoyed the meal, but the certainty of their own relationship even more.

Over coffee and a cognac, Barbara looked at her watch for the first time in the evening.

"Come on you; you have a board to dazzle in the morning – and me for a couple of hours first.

CHAPTER 20 - CASABLANCA, UPDIKE AND THE CALL TO ACCOUNT

Back at the apartment, the two of them fused together; there was no other description.

Their love making had a new intensity and passion with the pact of permanence there between them.

At the board meeting the next morning, the perceptive Tim could see the newly radiant Barbara.

"You look like a very happy woman this morning, if I may say."

"Hell yes, you may. Remember this moment, Tim, and I'll tell you all about it one day."

She had a new pride in *her* John.

He had rehearsed his ideas with her, and his long experience of getting a room on his side paid off completely.

The meeting may have started with a few board members harbouring doubts about what this incomer could bring; a short time later they were delighted that he was on the team.

He started by saying how honoured he was to be part of such a superb organisation and was delighted to be joining a board of such varied and world-class talent.

He praised them for their achievements so far, and their wisdom in spreading their activities way beyond petrochemicals and way beyond the UK.

If their original base markets ever weakened, they had massive strength in depth.

With them tuned in to him, he outlined where it could be even better; how work on individual and team presentation strategies could ensure that their message was strong and consistent – and profitable – and how it could be done.

He talked through the need to sharpen what they were doing on their well-accepted corporate responsibility role and their desire to have a respected charitable role.

He showed how they had wandered into a fragmented role – with many people in the company spending a lot of time on effectively trying to be charity managers – and having to turn down dozens of requests a week.

He put up a slide of a hit list of activity and structure. Nearly all those people who were swamped in activities which were really outside their expertise could be harnessed better in doing focussed work for the company.

MCP Global would form an alliance with a top charity well known to John. The charity's staff would manage the programmes and get it right. They would run the full package on governance, grant making and receiving, and the maze of activity which makes up a modern charity. Effectively, they would look after the engine room, and MCP would be the sleek ship above the water.

They would set up the MCP Foundation and achieve a worldwide reputation for quality.

They would create their own awards programme, and major events, to show the world they were the global leaders in every key business activity.

Barbara wondered if the other board members could hear her purring with pride.

He had absolutely dazzled them as she knew they would.

That was the start of another new world for John – as a key director and a celebrated business leader and innovator.

Another slice of novelty was beckoning too.

When the board meeting had ended, members went off to their various duties. It felt like the end of a successful speaking stint as they all, without exception, made a point of shaking John's hand and thanking him for a superb opening performance.

"We're clear for a couple of hours" said Barbara. "Let me get you back to the apartment so that I can thank you too."

"Before we do, a little treat for you."

She nodded to a very attractive young blonde lady, complete with pony tail.

"Come and join us Sally"

So, this was the lady who was John's travel guru; the one that Barbara had hinted had knowledge of their personal bond."

"As you know John, Sally is a very talented lady, but I want her to do even more for us – the three of us can be magic."

There was an electrical charge in the air.

"I want you to step up. Sally; you can appoint your successor to PA for John, but you'll still be working closely with John - and me.

I want John to guide you into that charitable role you've just been taking the minutes on.

John has created a new vision of just how big that could be for us – get a real hold of it Sally. We'll need a main board director to fulfil that role two years from now

– I want that person to be you."

She threw her arms around Barbara and John – and kissed them both as though she meant it.

"I can spot potential, can't I John? Do you know that Sally was eighteen just a few months ago – it's almost as if I could be her mother."

John gulped and managed to talk – some achievement given what Barbara had just planted in his head.

"Shall we say we'll have a coffee first thing tomorrow Sally and I can talk you through the new job?"

"I need to grab Barbara for a couple of hours right now – few things to discuss."

"Back at the apartment they discussed with major energy – mainly about Sally."

"Do you know what you do to me Barbara?"

"Hell, yes."

*****

Two years later, Sally was a main board director at the age of just over twenty.

Barbara and John had developed her as they had hoped. My word, they had.

It was also a day when, Barbara decided, she needed to move progress elsewhere.

It was also the day when Janet Bremner would receive the unforgettable phone call from accountant Brian.

John was indeed due to speak that evening in Park Lane – as host of a much anticipated MCP Global Foundation awards dinner.

The guest list would include major figures from

business and government ministers from six countries.

Barbara had asked him to catch the morning train and meet for an early lunch in her apartment.

The train was spot on time, London traffic was kind and the company driver was good.

Barbara opened the door and he kissed her hungrily.

Something felt different.

Taking a deep breath, she said. "I just want you to listen John. I'm terrified that I've done something wrong, but, please God, let it be right.

You are going to be receiving two phone calls soon – I caused them because I love you. I hope you'll love me for what I've done. If you hate me for it, I'll never forgive myself.

Brian your accountant will be ringing, even though he shouldn't, and Janet will be calling because she should."

John didn't take it all in, but, as he opened his mouth to speak, Barbara put her finger to his lips, then kissed them as she looked at her watch.

John's phone rang – it was Brian's number on the screen.

"John – this call never happened. I'm breaking client confidentiality and I could be struck off for that.

I act for both you and Janet personally, but this is a matter for her only and there's no way that I should be discussing this with you. But I have to."

"What the hell is going on Brian."

"Janet's coming in to see me shortly. I have a cheque here made payable to her for ten million pounds."

"Who from, and what the hell for?"

"It's from your friend Barbara – a personal cheque

mind, not company, and it has a small number of conditions – mainly that Janet raises no objection to you and Barbara being married."

John looked at Barbara; the room was so silent that she had heard the phone conversation clearly.

"Barbara's with you I presume" asked Brian.

"She is."

"I guess you have some talking to do. Janet will be here any minute and, remember, this call never happened."

All John could say to Barbara was "Why?"

"Do you remember that lovely day a couple of months ago when you were interviewed on the BBC about our Charity Awards and how they asked you what inspired you?"

"Of course, I do; what's that got to do with this?"

That piece from the John Updike book had me in tears and still does. I still have the transcript. Please, read it to me again. Please just do it – it will make sense. Just in case I've got all this wrong and my world explodes around me.

Reading those beautiful words would steady John's head and that was necessary right now.

In a steady, firm voice, he repeated the performance which had captivated a huge television audience. The interviewer had asked him where his own inspiration came from and, if the viewers were expecting something twee or ordinary, they were blown away by what John produced. He smiled at the interviewer and began;

One of my favourite writers is the American, John Updike, and when he died I felt as if I had lost a friend and a mentor. I love words and always tried to learn from him. He made you want to use the language as well as he did, but left you in the certain knowledge that you never could.

His last published work was a beautiful collection of short pieces called My Father's Tears and other Stories.

It was a fitting climax to a lifetime of shimmering skill.

He looks back on his youth at a fiftieth school reunion in a moving story called The Walk with Elizanne.

At the reunion he meets the girl in the story with whom he shared his first goodnight kiss at the age of fifteen.

He lost touch but remembers her telling him fifty years before, "We have tons of time."

If only.

Updike asks, and remember these are some of the last words he ever wrote;

"What does it mean; the enormity of having been children, and now being old, living next to death?"

He also describes the people he loves; "They can fill in the gaps between the words."

In the television interview, John paused and looked at the camera as the interviewer sat in reverent silence too.

In one newspaper review of the programme, John was described as "the man who made a nation hold its breath."

Now, John had an audience of one, and she was clearly affected all over again.

"Before you shout at me or hit me, or whatever I deserve, listen for one more minute.

After I'd heard you with those words from Updike, I was trying to recall something which had that kind of effect on me.

In the middle of the night, with you lying next to me, I remembered what it was.

Might not be as deep as John Updike, but still a classic.

It's from Casablanca, when Rick's talking to Ilsa;

If that plane leaves the ground and you're not with him, you'll regret it.

Maybe not today, maybe not tomorrow, but soon – and for the rest of your life.

I had to do this John, or we could have drifted into nothing. I need you for the rest of my life. If I had not been brave enough to do this, I would have regretted it for ever.

John's phone rang again; it was Janet.

THE END

(TO BE CONTINUED)

Acknowledgements

I've written much of this novel while travelling the world on the speaking circuit, and it's been quite something to recall some great memories while enjoying a view of a Caribbean sunset from my temporary office.

It's been lovely to look back on meeting some really special people who appear in the book, although some fictional names have appeared to protect the guilty.

The book is, of course, a work of fiction, and the characters and places come largely from my fertile imagination.

Warmest thanks to all who have helped with my debut novel and, in particular, to star mentor Chris Tarrant, and all at Michael Terence Publishing who have been so supportive in a world which is new to me.

There's more of what I do and novel updates on

www.afterdinnerspeakeralanwright.co.uk

- and there's a sequel on the way!"

———————

Available worldwide from

Amazon

———————

65528448R00123

Made in the USA
Middletown, DE
03 March 2018